THE
TORCH MASTER

Rev. Joseph A. Jensen Sr.

Gotham Books

30 N Gould St.
Ste. 20820, Sheridan, WY 82801
https://gothambooksinc.com/

Phone: 1 (307) 464-7800

© 2024 *Rev. Joseph A. Jensen Sr.* All rights reserved.

No part of this book may be reproduced, stored in a retrieval system, or transmitted by any means without the written permission of the author.

Published by Gotham Books (July 18, 2024)

ISBN: 979-8-88775-992-0 (P)
ISBN: 979-8-88775-993-7 (E)

Because of the dynamic nature of the Internet, any web addresses or links contained in this book may have changed since publication and may no longer be valid.

The views expressed in this work are solely those of the author and do not necessarily reflect the views of the publisher, and the publisher hereby disclaims any responsibility for them.

Table of Contents

PREVIEW - THE BOY v

INTRODUCTION - THE TORCH MASTER vi

CHAPTER ONE - THE CRASH 1

CHAPTER TWO - THE HIDDEN CITY 11

CHAPTER THREE - BIBLE STUDIES 21

CHAPTER FOUR - THE BOY AND THREE 25

CHAPTER FIVE - BEHIND THE FLAMES 30

CHAPTER SIX - THE TORCH MASTER 36

CHAPTER SEVEN - MISSIONS OF SORTS 43

CHAPTER EIGHT - TENT REVIVAL 50

CHAPTER NINE - THE HONEYMOON'S OVER 55

CHAPTER TEN - MAKING HISTORY 64

CHAPTER ELEVEN - THE PLAN 79

CHAPTER TWELVE - THE BIBLE 83

CHAPTER THIRTEEN - OUR SECRET WEAPON 89

PREVIEW

THE BOY

It had been five days since the blast and everyone was gone. The stench of death muddled with smoke filled the streets as seagulls fought over and picked at satchels left next to corpses, then suddenly they stopped. Alerted by movement they flew off a ways, and watched a bleeding hand clawing its way out of the rubble. It was only a short distraction before they landed and went back to fighting over things. A small fragile boy emerged from the debris. He was bleeding and moaning, in unsure surroundings, and unable to remember anything. He noticed birds fighting over a torn open satchel with some food pouring out of it. His hunger drove him to leap and grab it, then filling his mouth with its contents. The seagulls reluctantly watched him eat but, his eyes fixed on them as if they were going to be his next mouthful, so they kept their distance. He Ignored the smell and his own pain then began unwrapping corpses and dressing himself in their fine apparel. Then he harvested every satchel he could find. With his arms full

he buried his collection under stones taken from the walls of the broken fountain. The only wall that remained unscathed served as a base for a statue head, with water pouring out of its mouth the boy drank. The water wasn't pure it tasted a bit like oil. Still, he kept drinking until he was filled. As darkness came he lay up against a corpse and hugged it while falling asleep. He slept straight through the next day until the following morning. Then he woke up again from the sounds of seagulls fighting over and small objects or food. The boy grabbed his head in agony and moaned as he got up and walked down the street.

INTRODUCTION

THE TORCH MASTER

This story begins were most stories end. Disaster claimed their entire city. The surviving men with two old monks searched for victims for two days until the shelling returned. Then all efforts ended abruptly. They escaped into the jungle leaving a young twelve year old boy buried in the rubble of war undiscovered. The boy's name was Michael. He was the only child of missionaries that were headed to Japan when he was just six years old. Tragedy landed them in the ocean just off the Korean coastline, then into the gates of a hidden city. The discovery of it would turn out to be the first episode in a great, mystical journey, not only for him but many. The dreams of ten monks and fifteen families, the visions of a beautiful Priestess, and the records of a Head Monk that wrote every detail of them, would all become reality. And little Michael's destiny would be to live on to become a protector of those set behind the flames as a Torch Master.

Throughout this book there are twist and turns that will keep the reader in suspense. Love, romance, comedy, and horror surround each character. Their following adventures are all linked to fulfill a destiny. What destiny? God only knows. Our belief in God and heaven or nirvana in another life after death is common to all religions, but the hope for this world is not. While reading this story you may begin to feel as I do. That God may have seen enough violence someday to again intervene and force peace before we destroy ourselves. Though this story is fiction its hope is real.

CHAPTER ONE

THE CRASH

It was one of those classic hot sultry days known as dog days in the South. During these days of late summer people seldom stirred. Normally they sat under the shade of a porch, gazebo, or if nothing else a nice tree would suffice. But today was also Sunday and a day of thanksgiving. The heat was almost to the point of being unbearable. Nevertheless church was packed. Standing room only with twelve ceiling fans set on high. It was also a far cry from any typical day in Beaufort, South Carolina. Japan had just surrendered to the United State's and World War II was over. Everyone was smiling and rejoicing. Even the church service was better than ever. Pastor Paul stood proudly over the record turnout. He was an incredibly handsome man with dark hair and blue eyes. His wife Emily was also a beautiful woman with hazel eyes and long red hair. She stood shoulder height to her husband, but she hovered twice as tall over their little six year old son Michael. Being an only child and a pastor's son awarded him certain privileges. Michael learned at an earlier age that his mother was the least tolerant in the crowd. So at every chance he would slip away during service into some other yielding lap. Musical laps were his favorite game while his father gave his sermon. Michael also found out that a Chiclet of gum or candy were often the treats they used to settle his ambitions. Pastor Paul gave an incredible sermon. He told the story when he and Emily were college sweat hearts. Their colleagues often called Paul and Emily their Pentecostals who spoke in many tongues. Even though he studied Theology as a major both of them took language arts together and talked all the time about traveling. They were fluent in German, French, Spanish, Chinese, Japanese, and now learning Korean. He also spoke about the world and how it needed to be free from politics just like the church. He expressed, "All people are the same, everyone cries, laughs, eats, sleeps, lives and dies; the only thing that truly makes us different is being separated by distance." He then noted, "If we all lived together we would figure it out sooner or later and adapt to each other, because we are all the same." He continued on a little longer, filling everyone with the new hope of world peace.

After church Paul and Emily took their little six year old boy Michael to his first parade. Then later that night to a fireworks show. That whole week everyone celebrated with fireworks and dances. Even Pastor Paul and Emily danced like they had back in college. In fact Pastor Paul and Emily were somewhat famous in Tennessee, where they taught all their colleagues how to Shag. It was a South Carolina dance style that started in the thirties. They even taught little Michael how to Shag for fun and exercise. Only, two weeks later a group of the church leaders and the overseer came to visit Paul and Emily. They thought it was because they danced in public. Shagging wasn't considered by everyone to be the most respectful or clean form of dance. But they came to ask Paul and Emily to become ambassadors from the United States to help reconstruct Japan and restore the good nature of Americans. The overseer asked them not to rush into a decision. Leaving their church, friends, not to mention their country had to be the hardest choice and the most important decision in their lives. He left telling them he would fast and pray and encouraged them likewise to do the same.

A month later at Sunday service Pastor Paul announced their decision. Paul, Emily and little Michael were headed to Japan as missionaries. Paul and Emily were excited at first and little Michael was ecstatic, flying for the first time. He screamed out every five seconds," "Look mommy, look daddy" as he gazed out the window. But over the course of a week and the tedium of making several stops with plane changes turned his screams to "where we going or why?", or hollering, "I want to go home!" Reaching Hawaii they were completely in awe by the beauty and grandeur of the coastline. Although South Carolina had a beautiful shoreline as well, it was dwarfed in every aspect, even its climate. Their flight out was scheduled for later that week. So they planned to spend two days enjoying the beaches of Waikiki. During their stay Paul and Emily decided to see Pearl Harbor. Once there Paul was taken aback by the immensity of the destruction when Japan attacked Dec.7, 1941. He had never seen war or its destruction close up. Despite his noble profession being a pastor from South Carolina, he never took part or agreed with any war. Praying with his wife Emily and Michael he asked God, "Can this kind of hatred people have towards one another ever make sense? They never knew each other!" Anguished he continued, "Why are we about to go to Japan to aid them in their recovery efforts and leaving our own country to get well?" Overwhelmed by emotions Paul fell to his knees and cried, while experiencing a divine revelation. His thoughts were rehearsing their lives like a sermon preaching to his mind. Why they both ended up in the same Bible College at the same time was no coincidence.

They had been predestined to do this job. Those years studying together and learning languages with their ministry resembled perfectly shaped puzzle pieces being crafted and manipulated into place by a master designer. Both of them graduated with honors in 1938. Paul graduated a PhD in Theology with a minor degree in Language Arts. Emily graduated a PhD in Language Arts and a minor degree in Theology. Emily was the true driving force for Paul to learn languages which became the glue that held them together. They often played word or geographical games about traveling and working as missionaries as their lives ambition. While playing those games they always quoted the Bible verse in every language they knew, "Go and teach all nations the Gospel of Jesus Christ." Both of them were virtually unprepared now for this type of reality as they looked upon the devastation. Their only thought was what lied ahead of them. Whether or not God lead them to this point or just taking advantage of the circumstances that placed them together, they knew without a doubt it was His purpose for them to get on the plane and go.

They left Hawaii in a old C-47 ex- military cargo plane loaded with medical supplies and provisions. The pilot, co- pilot and navigator were the only others on board. Their flight schedule too, were extremely rigorous, long and uncomfortable.

Not to mention problems with the plane only made Paul and Emily that much more apprehensive. Their first stop in Wake was very brief. It stopped only long enough to get fueled before heading to Okinawa. Their scheduled plans were to fuel and go from there also, then fly straight to Tokyo, Japan, but once the plane was fueled up in Okinawa it encountered electrical problems which kept it from starting again. The pilot then made matters worse, not thinking of his audience, shouting out, "That's why these planes were called gooney birds." Immediately, Paul cleared his throat. The pilot turned around and looked at them before telling his navigator, "Why don't you help this family go out to stretch their legs in the fresh morning air while we work on the plane."

Once outside, reminders of the war littered the sides of the runway with remnants of broken planes and abandoned equipment. Little Michael was all keyed up and rambunctious just wanting to play in all the junk. Unlike Paul and Emily who were nervous over the planes condition, also knowing this was the last stop before reaching Japan. Thirty minutes later the plane started and everyone got back on board. They flew all day and through most of the night. Michael slept in his father's lap until early morning when Paul gently got up and put Michael into his mother's arms next to the window and placed a blanket over them. Afterwards Paul stretched on the floor and went to sleep. As they slept the electrical systems malfunctioned causing them to fly off course over the Sea of Japan towards Korea. Paul woke up to the the pilots call "S.O.S. this is flight …." Over and over he repeated his message with their coordinates. Quickly, Paul grabbed Michael and placed him beneath himself as he told Emily to stay strapped in and bend over with her head in her lap. Seconds later their plane hit the water with a force great enough to tear the front of the plane completely away with the pilot and his crew. Emily was barely able to move when she heard Michael screaming with his father lying on top of him, unconscious. As the water rushed in Emily screamed out to Paul while unbuckling herself. In her panic she pulled Paul off little Michael and grasp her screaming child up. Just then Paul groaned and moved as the water rushed over his head. Emily screamed, "Are you okay?" And Paul replied, "Yes, I'll be alright!" He then prayed over and over, "God help us," as he struggles to get them out of the aircraft. Afterwards, he went back in it and found a raft in the planes emergency compartment and swam out pulling it through the debris.

Once he reached them he frantically placed Michael and Emily safely into the raft as he floated beside it. Watching the plane sink out of sight in the glare of moonlight, they had mixed emotions. Had God abandon them or delivered them? They floated in the ocean all morning and most of the following day. Then two hours before sunset the rocky shoreline unveiled itself. They could see in the distance a beach surrounded by high cliffs covered with vines. Excitedly, Paul swam pulling the raft towards a coves shoreline. They were soon close enough to hear the waves pounding it's beach. The sounds helped Emily and little Michael forget their situation. But Paul, while he was pulling their raft through the waves was noticing the disappearing shoreline. The tide was coming in too fast, this meant big trouble. While pressing through the waves Paul instructed, "Emily! get ready to quickly grab little Michael to get out of the raft as fast as you can." Once they reached the shallows Paul immediately helped Emily and Michael disembark the raft. Then he pulled the raft to the widest part of the beach in a cove. Emily and Michael sat together shivering and whimpering as Paul marked a line in the sand. Then he said, "Stay close to the raft and watch the tide, and if the tide reaches this line, Emily you need to float back out." He continued his warning in Japanese so little Michael would not understand, "Emily go out far enough so that the tide won't carry the raft back in to crash against the cliffs. I can always swim back out to get you again."

After Paul explained he hurriedly left them with a hug and kiss saying, "God will keep you safe, I love both of you" and started climbing the cliff to seek help. Little Michael and his mother watched Paul as he struggled to scale the rock face, tugging on vines that broke on his way up. Then half way up he slipped again before grabbing another vine. As he pulled it from a crevasse it revealed a pipeline made of bamboo that was concealed within the cliff. At the top was a bamboo jungle. Paul's eyes followed the pipelines path to tall stone walls partially camouflage in vines. As he approached a fortress Paul heard voices, so he screamed out "Help me, please help me!" in Japanese. But the voices inside said, "Toru tanita", meaning go around in Korean. Paul did not have a clue what they were saying, But, he followed the voices until he found the front gates opened up by four men. Also, two old monks were holding back a crowd. Everyone was asking Paul questions in Korean and Paul only recognized one word 'Maengse' meaning oath. The monks were to busy holding the back crowd and repeating "oath." Paul had no choice but find a twig and write on the ground in Big Korean Letters, "HELLO, MY WIFE AND SON ARE ON THE BEACH BELOW IN DANGER AS THE TIDES IS COMING IN FAST."

Then Paul took off. The younger of the two old monks gave chase. As the other old monk tapped several men to follow. Paul ran to the cliff and climbed back down to Emily and Michael jumped into Paul's arms. While the geezer monk finally read Paul's message. He slapped his head then ran to the cliffs edge, too. Then he ordered everyone to bring him vines as he started weaving a rope. As Paul had Michael in his arms his pursuers reached him speaking Korean. Emily hollered to them in perfect Korean, "Stop chasing my husband and grab the raft it's floating away." The water was covering their feet. By the time they saved the raft, the old monk threw down a long rope made of vines. Paul had Michael hug him tight with the rope tied around them and under his armpits. Emily say "No way Paul. You're not going to crush Michael again." Then Paul told Emily to tell the Korean men to make a daisy chain to pass Michael up the cliff. "Have them call for more men to come down from above to pass Michael up. After Michael's up you can tie the rope around yourself for safety and climb up with their help. I will tie the raft on to be pulled up next. Then they can pass me the rope to tie around me for safety as I climb up." After Emily told them and the Korean men were in place they passed Michael up. Emily went up next. Then the raft, finally Paul reached the top. By that time the cove was filled in a ten foot sea. At the top, the old monk asked Emily if there were any more survivors. Emily says in perfect Korean, "No, our plane crashed and the pilot and crew were lost." The elder monk said, "bae," meaning "ship". Emily says, "No, bihaeng giga eobada" meaning "No airplane." He scratch his head, the repeated, "bae" Emily says, "No, bihaeng giga eobada." As Emily followed the monks the old monk kept questioning Emily saying, "bae" while Michael rode on his fathers shoulders to the temple. It never occurred to Emily no one there ever heard, seen, or learned of an airplane. Paul, Emily, and little Michael had literally entered the Twilight Zone.

Though the people in the Hidden City never heard or saw a plane, they never heard off or saw this either. Were they missing anything as everything was built with stone or bamboo? They never saw a car, motorcycle, or a bicycle either. But, they never needed them, nor steel and aluminum. This junk will be recycled maybe into guns, ammunition, and equipment to fight another war. Martial Artist train with Bamboo that is natural and is it's stronger than steel and lighter than aluminum and seldom leaves more than a bruise, plus it's FREE.

CHAPTER TWO

THE HIDDEN CITY

Once both monks led them up the stairs and into the temple, the younger monk took Emily and Michael straight to the spa. As the elder monk held Paul back. He was constantly talking but Paul did not understand a word he said. Paul studied script of all the languages before he learned to speak or understand it. He could read and write anything in Korean, and many languages including Egyptian hieroglyphics and Sanskrit. But, he hadn't learned to understand or speak Korean yet. Emily's excuse for Paul to others was he didn't have an ear for words, like some do not have and ear for music. Yet he was a calligrapher. So, the old monk left Paul alone in the front of the temple and Paul did not know why unless it was to give him and Emily some privacy. So, he stripped naked. The old monk was telling Paul he was going after towels, robes, and sandals. So, he could take them to them. Instead, when the the old monk came back with everything Paul was butt naked and motioning for a pen and paper. The old monk took Paul as being a perverted Frankenstein coming after him and threw everything up in surprise and ran away. Paul just shrugged and put on the robe and sandals. Afterwords picked everything up trying to separate clean and dirty in diffident arms, even his mouth. Once he had everything Paul followed the sandy trail to hear Emily and Michael laughing. They were splashing each other in a hot spa. When Paul opened the door Michael splashed him. Paul quickly put all the clean dry stuff on the bench then jumped in with everything else, in his robe, and sandals. This started a wet clothes fight. Little Michael got out and threw all their their clothes in, even their sandy shoes. A while later the younger of the old monks returned. Paul and Emily were just finishing wringing all the clothes. At his knock Emily invited him in. At his first glance he noticed the stack of washed clothes, their wet shoes, Paul's wet wallet, keys, watch, and some lose coins. He had more towels, Emily's sandals, Michaels clothes, also ink, paper and a quill. Plus, a letter, where the old monk wrote about their ordeal.

Then he asked Emily if he could take the wet stuff and he said he would come back with another dry robe for Paul. Emily of course politely agreed and thanked him in perfect Korean. After the monk left Paul got out then read the letter. The old monk apologized for running away throwing their towels and robes. Also, for worrying more about the peoples oath. Then wrote hot food would be waiting for them in the dinning room after their bath with a map to get to the dinning. Paul wrote they were headed to Japan after the World War II was over. Japan surrendered May 8, 1945. Germany surrendered September 2, 1945. Paul stopped because Michael got out and wanted to draw. Paul started teaching Michael to draw with a quill pen and ink at three year olds. Being a picture is worth a thousand words Paul let Michael start his own drawing. Michael drew a picture of the plane flying over the Hawaiian Islands. The younger old monk came back with another robe and sandals before Paul could write more. Paul handed him his unfinished letter with Michaels drawing anyway. The monk turned his back to Paul to let change robes and sandals. The second he read it the monk crushed it with Michaels drawing and left.

Emily screamed, "Paul, what did you just write." When Paul told her. Emily screams, "Paul, did it ever occur to you in Korea, they have been under Japanese rule since last century and by the looks of this place nothing changed. I doubt these people know what a bicycle is, let alone a car, or airplane.

You just told them we defeated two countries even the whole world. How can we explain they're not going to be next. Paul are you trying to get another PhD for Stupidity?"

Paul got Michaels clothes and a towel, his ink, paper and quill then left with Michael naked. Emily screamed crying, "Come back, come back Paul, please come back!"

Paul went to the dining room to pray and calm down. He took his time drying and dressing Michael as he prayed. Prayer always helped Paul the most so it wasn't long before he and Michael were making Emily an apology card. Michael drew them holding hands under a Cross and lots of X's and O's for hugs and kisses.

Emily followed the map to find Paul and Michael and she found them as Micheal and Paul were finishing his apology card. Then it was a grand reunion as their cries turned to laughs. Together as a family they voiced another favorite in harmony, "God only knows what's going to happen next." Yet, they did know because the smell of hot steaming food rose from the edges of baskets, with a cloth napkin wrapped around chopsticks lay in the ring handle of three separate kimchi pots. They ate and until the monks came back with a woman. The older monk introduced himself as Woo jin and apologized again to Paul. Eun ji introduced himself but he was still upset and would not apologize not even to little Michael.

However, Woo jin apologized for Eun ji speaking to Emily, "I'm so sorry for Eun ji crumpling your sons picture I hope the hot food was pleasant. Have you and the boy eaten enough?" Emily replied in perfect Korean, "Yes, thank you, we enjoyed the hot meal and we are all full." Then Woo jin asked, "Will you please allow this woman to care for your son and let him play with the other children. Meanwhile, we may talk with you and your husband." Emily was hesitant, but let little Michael go, telling him, "Be nice and don't fight."

Once Michael had gone, Paul started to ask Emily to interpret his apology and explanation, but the Elder monk put finger to his lips, then he pointed up, lastly to himself, then back up again. Paul interpreted to Emily asking, "Did he just say, 'Shut up, and let me talk first.' or he's number one?" Emily says, "Yep, that pretty much what he said, without saying a word."

Then Woo jin says, "Please, keep eating more as I explain. No one had ever come to this city since it started seventy two years ago. In fact no one knows this city even exist. Seventy five years ago we were part of a group of ten monks who planned to build this hidden city because of war. Our leader Kwan Lee was very careful in choosing this location, trying to keep the distance from wars and the politics that created them."

Eun ji stated, "This city wasn't meant to be great but rather hidden by the bamboo jungle and tall cliffs above the ocean, which made it virtually inaccessible. We built these tall walls to keep the world out and our world in. Over time vines covered the walls making it more obscure. The politics of war or nations never entered our cities gates. In fact, no one even knew what was outside of the walls, except us and a few elders. Everyone else was raised here from birth and never has been out of this city. We knew our children and people often talked about a world outside, in secret but they have never seen or heard anyone from beyond these walls until you came."

Woo jin continues, "Seventy five years ago we were the two youngest monks. I was nineteen Eun ji was sixteen. Our leader Kwan Lee started debates that questioned the politics within our own religion. All monks in the monastery were highly trained martial artist. Kwan

Lee was the best Master under Grand Master Hyun Shik our Head Monk. No matter, the people or our Emperor Jose-son never let us know of an invasion. So, we could not to defend the victims of war or give them shelter. Due to a lack of concern. Kwan Lee left the monastery to get answers. Kwan Lee returned to the monastery three months later to tell our Head Monk Hyun Shik and us about the invasion at the Gateway of Ganghwa Strait. This started an uprising. Seven monks left with Master Kwan Lee. We wanted to leave too. But, Master Kwan Lee told us to stay and wait. He promised to come back for us."

Eun ji said, "Kwan Lee did not come back because they were searching for a place to build this city outside of this world. While we were waiting we had to listen to the other monks calling us rebels, fanatics, and a leaders of a new cult."

Woo jin continues, "Kwan Lee and the seven monks dreams were to build the perfect place as heaven with no problems, tranquil, bliss, like nirvana. Over a long period Kwan Lee with seven monks finally found this location. After that they recruited fifteen families to help build the city and they would start the foundation for new generations. Those families were all told wait and get everything ready to meet up with all their provisions: food, tools, clothing and animals and everything needed to build this new city hidden from the world. Three years passed when Kwan Lee secretly sneaked back in the monastery to get us. The other monks were sent earlier to get the families, when we all met for the first time. Then Kwan Lee led us on a very secret exodus to this site."

Eun ji said, "That night was the last time anyone every spoke of the world or returned to it. It took seventy two years to build this hidden city the way you see it now. We are the only two monks left from those first ten monks. Some of the elders were part of the original families that came too. But, everyone including every monk took a sworn oath that we would never disclose any knowledge of the hidden city to the out outside nor pass on any knowledge of the outside to anyone inside, including their own children."

Paul was astonished from what they just heard and he needed to find out their new position as prisoners, followers, or allowed to leave without disclosing the secrets of the hidden city.

But right now Emily wanted to find her child and seek shelter, privacy, and sleep.

The monks had already sensed her weariness and they had arranged things. Both monks asked Paul and Emily to please follow them. They led them to a house in the center of the city. Little Michael was playing in front with the other children while everyone cleaned their new home up and decorated it by placing gifts of food, blankets, linen, clothing, even built a fire to welcome them in. Paul and Emily were in tears while they hugged and thanked everyone. Michael still wanted to play more with his new friends, but Emily insisted that he come inside to sleep and tell them, "kamsahamnda annyonghi jumushipsiyo" meaning thank you and good night in Korean. Michael just reiterated, "Thank you, thank you, and good night."

The following morning everyone was waiting for Paul, Emily, and little Michael to wake up and join them for breakfast. The crowd led them to an open patio with a large kitchen next to the temple. Under the shelter were short tables for dining and everyone brought a bamboo mat to kneel on. Both monks were there to greet them, bowing first then leading them to their places. Their mats were already set down for them at the front table. Food set steaming in bamboo baskets with covered lids. Everyone else formed a line and received their own basket with inviting smells of morning egg omelet. with bean sprouts, broccoli, and tender bamboo shoots, added. As they all past by to receive their own basket they bowed to Paul, Emily, and little Michael before the knelt down in their places. Then Woo jin blessed the food as the Eun ji continually bowed while he prayed. Paul stood up and said in English, "May God bless this food we are about to receive in Jesus name." Emily replied, "Amen" as she did not know the translation for 'Amen'. The people were all waiting for them to take their first bites and Emily said again, "Amen", she would not take a bite of food until everyone replied "Amen." So, they finally said, "Amen." Little Michael was so short he stood up to eat and thought he was eating from a playhouse table. He just laughed and ate, while making funny gestures to get all the other children laughing.

After breakfast Paul was invited to take a tour of the city and left with the two old monks. Emily stayed with the women to clean the dining area as elders took the children to play. Emily knew it was hard for them not to ask so she invented ways to change the subject like telling their stories. The Bible was a serious book of violence. These people never learned of Moses, Samson, David and Goliath, or war. They never conceived violence, slavery, or cruelty. It would would be a sin if Emily or Paul revealed these things. They could not reveal the Bible. Neither could Emily tell them most of their own stories. So, they talked about the children, families, and weather.

Meanwhile Paul marveled as they walked through the city. He was amazed by their craftsmanship, engineering and even technology. The city itself was built over natural springs. Originally a waterfall flowed into the ocean before it was dammed for their water and piped into two paths. The first path was for drinking the water that was tapped to everyone's home and building. The other was a source for pure water into the fountain at city square. They put drain in the fountain to allow the old water out into channels that constantly flowed under every house for sewage that was piped to the garden and rice field. But the most ingenuous part of their whole system was that they even piped in hot water from natural hot springs from high mountains using bamboo coated with dry lime cement. Every house and the temple had plenty of hot water to heat and bathe in. The fountain had a way to blend hot and cold water to wash clothes and the temple even had hot spa for the monks. Stones brought up from the high the cliffs overlooking the ocean were used to build everything. The tall city walls, the temple, and every house were made of rock brought up from the waterfalls pool in the cove before fresh water met the sea. At the end of the city, opposite the temple was a farm with animals and gardens and a rice field where all the men worked each day. Also, fruit trees of every kind, and huge evergreen oaks for wood. Twice a day the monks blessed food prepared from the garden and farm animals in the outside kitchen. There was a community center that served as a daycare where elderly woman watched the children while the spun wool, or silk, or made clothes or tapestry. It also served as a indoor kitchen and place to eat when it was cold or rained and a community center. The city was self-sufficient and ran like a Swiss watch, but Paul knew he had to either leave or start witnessing to fulfill his calling. So he asked the monks if they would take him back into the temple to talk. But, Paul would not talk he would write. Paul wrote then was a holy man of God and he needed to leave or start a church there. Both monks were less concerned about his God, than they were about them leaving. They knew they could never let them leave. Then Woo jin said, "Tell us about your God," and Paul started writing the Gospel when Eun ji stopped him and asked, "Why does your God not stop wars that bring division between men?" Then Paul without thinking wrote, "Sometimes war is necessary." Both monks were startled, and so was Paul. What did war accomplish? For the first time Paul had to defend war. He wrote, "If evil came to you, all of this you will have to fight for or give up and become slaves." He wrote, "This is your life, and it is your right to keep it the way it is. But evil claims everything and if it came here today you have to fight for your life to keep it the way you made it."

The Eun ji was furious and hit the table hard with his fist. Paul's Bible fell of and the ink spilled. Eun ji said in Korean, "I knew this might happen read this!" Then Eun ji handed Paul a letter. Eun ji wrote, "Our leader was Master Kwan Lee. He left the monastery seeking answers. Then every three months he came back to tell Head Monk Hyun Monk Hyun Shik and the other monks what happened. We both remember the first time Kwan Lee came with news that he wrote. We still have his pages and secretly read them from time to time. Kwan Lee wrote, 'An American gunship named, USS General Sherman came by way of the Yellow Sea to the Strait of Ganghwa followed by two Chinese Junks. When approached by Korean Officials in an official boat an interpreter named Reverend Thomas Brown hollered to them he was a friend of Emperor Jose-son and they came baring gifts. Reverend Brown invited authorities onboard. Starting their search the immediately uncovered the ships forward cannon. Below other authorities found many sealed crates, When the head authority insisted the crates be opened the ships Captain pulled out his gun the Reverend told them the ship was loaded with more cannon, modern guns, and gun powder. The ship's Captain by the owner named Preston shot the head officer as the crew shot the other officials. The Chinese too fired on the Garrison as the gunship shot their cannon. The Chinese shot their way into the fort to kill twenty soldiers. Afterwards, they proceeded up the Taedong River to reach Pyongyang and Emperor Jose- son. Later that day Korean Officials set mines in the river and it stopped the ships. Korean Officials came to Preston's Gunship again by boat under a white flag. Again the owner nod to allow them aboard. Preston told Reverend Thomas Brown to tell the weapons and this ship came from another war in America. Whereby, they were losing. We were part of a Confederacy of thirteen states against twenty five states. Yet they held then off thee years. We lost our families and friends, and homes. You know too they took slaves from Shanghai for forty years. This is why Emperor Jose-son had the Gangwha Garrisons built, so their slave ship would not come to Pyongyang to defeat Emperor Jose-on. Then take Koreans as slaves as they did the Chinese. The Chinese with me have been fighting the Americans slave ships those forty years, while we fought our war against them too for three years. They are coming here right now, I figured before I lose my war with them these weapons might save some in our position. Now you have to decide. If these weapons and gunpowder don't reach Emperor Jose-son and you lose your country like I lost mine you are the one responsible. Then head Official told Reverend Thomas Brown said Korean, "if what you said about being Emperor Jose-son was true and the are gifts then come with us alone to see Emperor Jose- son. Preston agreed to let Reverend Thomas go as he did not know where they mined the river or if it was a bluff. He only knew he had the heaviest ship filled with gunpowder and arms'."

This was all Kwan Lee wrote. Paul's tried to write but he had no ink and he was scared. He ran out to get Emily, she had to no idea what happened but Paul brought Emily to the office and Eun ji was standing on the Bible opened on the floor with the spilled ink. She screamed at Paul even tried to get Eun ji foot off the Bible at no avail. Then Paul shaking told Emily to interpret everything he says word for word. Paul started, "Those soldiers killed at Gangwha Gate were not Korean's they were Japanese. It too bad Kwan Lee did not come back five years later. Because I can tell you why he knew everything they said. You said he built this city because they brought beheaded bodies to the monastery to the Chunchon monastery to be cremated. Your standing on the providence of the book that brought you and us to this hidden city. Kwan Lee was there for the same reason, We are here talking about this. Kwan Lee was there because he tried to find out what happened. He found out the Japanese were everywhere and after the Royal Japanese Emperor was killed their leader proclaimed he was now Imperial Emperor of the Japanese. Then he ordered every monk and Samurai shot from a distance then beheaded every head was laid before him. This Imperial Emperor was as Evil as anyone could get. He is the one who named himself a god and Imperial Emperor. Because he formed an army with modern weapons. When Kwan Lee came back he found the monks heads on poles in ever city. You were in Chunchon Monastery had the Japanese reached it all of you would have been beheaded including Kwan Lee. So he went North to Pyongyang where he learned of this from a letter written by Reverend Thomas Brown. Reverend Brown was the only white man allowed in Korea for ten years because he lived in Pyongyang and taught Emperor Jose-son about everything including our war, the slaves, and the strength of your armies. Emperor Jose-son. They were good friends. So Emperor Jose-son sent Reverend Thomas Brown back with his Elite monks to interpret if the weapons were truly meant for him and a gift he was to tell them to leave the ship with weapons and go back with the Chinese. Once Reverend Thomas Brown got back with the monks it was gone. So, seven bowman and fourteen monks with swords on each side of river followed the Taedong upstream with Reverend Brown. Soon they they could see the two Chinese Junks coming back. With the monks lined on each side and bows draw Reverend Brown ask what happened. As junks Captain and the men in both junks men kept very still. He said, "Preston ship was upstream and stranded aground as he kept the heavy vessel to close to bank to avoid the mines. It broke a paddle wheel and it was disabled. He also said we did not want to come this far." Reverend Brown said, "remember if was with you a Gangwha Strait when you guys had no problem killing everyone there. And you don't have those weapon or gunpowder otherwise you would have simply shot us. Which leads me to believe Preston's ship is gone. Probably by a mine. And you came this far to steal his cargo. The Captain started to draw hid gun and all the Chinese crews killed in seconds. Then they set both junks on fire cremating every before the ships sank out of sight.

Just then ji hit the table he states, "Then you come here with evil?" Paul then closed telling Emily to interpret. "We are leaving. If Kwan Lee made it here, we can make it there. Both of you are old and you can't stop us. We are not Evil. We are still fighting the Japanese here in Korea because the people do not know what I told you. They lived so long with the Japanese they live as gods above those in the North who live like dogs. But this fight as you two were once being trained was yours, I use to hate wars but the only reason evil spreads is the people at first live in fear and necessity. Then they are rewarded over time and given, food, land, and nice things. Because they lost their souls, we have to go because the book your starting contains the words from God just as I told you. Everyone in North Korea knows Reverend Thomas Brown because he was a true friend of Emperor Joseon. What I see here you're hiding. You can't hide God or from God.

Eun ji cried, and Woo said, "Please write your Bible before you go in Korea. We will get you paper and you can have your church in here this building, this can be your office. Then if you decide to leave as you said, we can't stop you."

Looking up to God, Paul prayed with his hands out stretch in perfect Korean said, "So, this is it, we're not in Japan we're here. I can't understand or speak Korean but I can read and write it. Everything Emily and I learned from books and we can't answer simple questions. I know You're here. You walk ahead of us, behind us, over us. Your in us creating Your own journey. You know what is going to happen next. Because you're leading our next step. Making everything work out. No matter what we do wrong You make it right. Thank You God. I am honored to stay and write You're words in Korean."

Woo Jin, Eun ji, and Emily did not know whether to cry, laugh, even move as this was not like speaking in tongues. Paul's prayer was in perfect Korean and he did not realize it until the monks told him in Korean.

Below is the USS General Sherman

CHAPTER THREE

BIBLE STUDIES

Paul's set a goal for himself to write at least one page a day. Because he was a calligrapher and a scribe he had to make sure ever word was the same. So he had to establish a reference to define words as Amen. The pages were also beautiful. But, transcribing his Bible was a joy rather then explaining it. They still came to Paul with questions. Even with a PhD he stumbled hard for words to explain it. These monks were far from being ignorant or naive. The monks waited on Paul to take breaks to eat or rest then Woo jin asked Paul alone, "How could God create a greater light to day and a lesser light to rule the night on the first day and do the same thing on the forth day?" Other times these two monks ganged up on Paul and pick up at Woo jin who always ask the first question or questions, "Why did God not just destroy Adam and Eve in the beginning after they conceived evil that would contaminate their offspring?"

Eun ji then asked Paul before he could answer Woo jin, "Was it wiser for God to wait and watch evil spread, than destroy all of nature he created later by a flood?" He added. "Were all those animals, plants, and trees He destroyed evil too?"

Then Woo jin asked, "Do not children love and respect their father because he loves them and protects them? And why did God succumb the serpent and allowed it to destroy His children's innocence? Did God not know this serpent was in his garden an allowed His children to go into a snare? Or was this serpent craftier and circumvented his way through His garden without detection? Either way was this the fault of the children? Do we not love and respect our children and expect our father to love us and protect us, not destroy us?"

Paul really couldn't answer and thought to himself in prayer, "Oh God, why aren't you here to defend yourself, I am totally unequipped for these kinds of questions." When Paul went home every evening he was worn out from the questions, when they weren't asking Paul they were asking Emily, her observations were as Paul's they were teaching them. They always reasoned between themselves why God did the things He did, and then they were commending God for His tolerance and compassion. God was in fact becoming their main focus. The monks started coming to his house before breakfast to get whatever he finished the night before. They were very impressed with many of the people that followed God like Moses seem to be like Kwan Lee who led their exodus to build the hidden city. They even discussed other alternatives which sometimes led to debates. When this happened they went to find Paul maybe Emily to referee or explain. It was very fulfilling for Paul as he listened to them analyze the Bible. This went on everyday like clockwork. Even the monks started going to church every morning after breakfast and sang hymns, clapped, or bowed depending on the spirit within them. One thing for sure, their focus on God had been changing them towards becoming His fans.

After three years immersed in the hidden city Michael spoke and understood Korean as well as his mother. Paul actually understood and spoke clear in Korean just as he gave his sermon on VJ Day when he said, "If everyone had to live together they would adapt to each other." Paul was planning to finish the last pages the night before Michaels ninth Birthday. No one knew not even Emily or Michael. Because neither of them took time to learn to read or write Korean. Then on Michaels Birthday Paul handed the monks his last pages. After they read them they asked Paul to let them preach the Bible from what they had learned and figured out. But Paul's answer to them was, "You need to be baptized first." The monks were honored and bowed, then the Woo jin asked Paul, "When?" Paul exclaimed, "Right now!" They bowed to Paul again, and proceeded to the fountain. Paul climbed into the water first, followed by Woo jin. As Paul placed one of his hands behind the Woo Jin's back and the other behind his head, he said in perfect Korean. "Do you believe that Jesus Christ is the Son of God who became a living sacrifice for the forgiveness of our sins and then resurrected from dead and now sits at the right hand of God?" The Woo jin replied, "I do". Then Paul continued and said, "By your profession of Jesus Christ to be the risen Son of God, I now baptize you in name of the Father, and of his Son Jesus Christ, and the Holy Ghost." Then Paul dunked him underwater and he emerged holding his hands high in the air praising Jesus. Afterwards the Eun ji jumped in and was baptized, all morning and afternoon all the people of the city were baptized including their still tiny son Michael. It was a day to remember with everyone standing around the fountain with their hands raised worshiping Jesus. Paul proclaimed this day to be celebrated as Baptism Day and it would be everyone's birthday in Christ. Paul also announced his new deacons were now monks of God and would be preaching and teaching the Bible. Over the next three years, life went on with a new sequence of events starting with morning church, then breakfast, and then work. They never disclosed war or violence except in their version of the Gospel sparing a lot of graphic details. Both Paul and Emily agreed with the monks early on that it would be more harmful than good for them to learn of these things. Then the day came when their serenity was shaken by bombs exploding far off. At first they were taken as thunder even by the monks and the elders who merely forgot their sounds. As the war came closer their sounds were unmistakable with their constant roar to bring back bad memories. They realized it was only short time before their city would be discovered. The world was pounding at its doors, inevitably they would be broken to challenge their way of life. Paul, Emily, the elders, and monks all knew what was going to happen next. Their peace and way of life as they have known it was ending. It was the ending to their dream of a peaceful society, hidden from all wars and politics. It was too late for anyone to tell these innocent children that they were now going to become slaves to a brutal world. At first, when the bombs exploded away from the city the small children quit playing in the streets and ran into to laps of the elders. The elders made up stories about the thunder and reverted to their old beliefs saying, "The little god's are arguing over little things as little children". As they shared the story, they mocked the little god's with funny gestures. Then they said, "When Father God spanked those little gods, that lightning was his fury." The children all laughed after the story and mocked the little gods, as well. But as days went by, the bombing came closer and shook the stone walls, everyone was terrified. Just then a bomb exploded just beyond walls, and they crumbled. Paul and Emily beckoned all the women, children, and elderly, into their church. All of the men ran towards the temple when a bomb burst right on top of the church. In that frantic moment it was like time stood still, the noise deafened their ears, stopped their hearts, and footsteps. The men all ran back with the monks to uncover the bodies hoping to find someone alive. The pain of losing their families was far greater as the men dug. They ignored any physical pain and became numb. But everyone in the church was lost. Over the next two days they struggled to find their buried love ones and prepare them. The monks ordered all the bodies wrapped in their finest clothes and linen and laid next to the fountain with satchels of food for their trip to next life. There search ended when the shelling came back almost destroying the fountain in city square. Those exploding bombs forced all the men and two monks to abandon their efforts to cremate the water soaked bodies and left into the jungle. The two old monks told the men about the world that they were now going to live in. Ending their words, Woo jin said, "We must all split up in small groups of two or three to avoid detection. Jesus said, 'Where two or three are gathered in my Name, I will be there also.'" Then the Eun ji said, "Go now into the world and preach the Gospel of Jesus Christ."

CHAPTER FOUR

THE BOY AND THREE

It had been five days since the blast and everyone was gone. The stench of death muddled with smoke filled the streets as seagulls fought over and picked at satchels left next to corpses, then suddenly they stopped. Alerted by movement they flew off a ways, and watched a bleeding hand clawing its way out of the rubble. It was only a short distraction before they landed and went back to fighting over things.

A small fragile boy emerged from the debris. He was bleeding and moaning, in unsure surroundings, and unable to remember anything. He noticed birds fighting over a torn open satchel with some food pouring out of it. His hunger drove him to leap and grab it, then filling his mouth with its contents. The seagulls reluctantly watched him eat but, his eyes fixed on them as if they were going to be his next mouthful, so they kept their distance. He Ignored the smell and his own pain then began unwrapping corpses and dressing himself in their fine apparel. Then he harvested every satchel he could find. With his arms full he buried his collection under stones taken from the walls of the broken fountain. The only wall that remained unscathed served as a base for a statue. With water pouring out of its mouth the boy drank. The water wasn't pure it tasted a bit like oil. Nevertheless, he kept drinking until he was filled. As darkness came he lay up against a corpse and hugged it while falling asleep. He slept straight through the next day until the following morning when he woke up again from the sounds of seagulls fighting over small objects or food. The boy grabbed his head in agony and moaned as he got up and walked down the street. He was headed towards the temple which still stood above the rest of the broken city. One staircase was gone the other intact without damage. After climbing the steps he reached the doorway blocked by debris from the broken porch covering. Around the side he found a small window and climbed through. The dark open space had an inviting glare across the room. As he crossed the room he slid down on the slick polished floors.

When he got up he noticed a simmering light shining from a vessel at the base of a statue. The statue had a similar look to the statue at the fountain and he stared at it for the longest time then asked it in Korean,

"Who are you?" It never answered but the boy felt as if it were a friend or family member. The boy made several trips that day to bring back everything he had stashed and whatever he could find. That night he curled up next to the statue and slept only to be awakened by the roar of bombs bursting close by. Filled with fear he ran to the front doors and opened them. He took the broken boards from the collapsed porch to cover up every window, then blocked up the door, again. He stayed inside for days and had cut off all the circulation of fresh air. When the flames from the fire gradually smoldered soot filled the temple with large webs of smoldering ash and a thick haze. His body was a mere skeleton and his skin and garments blacken by the soot. He resorted to scavenging like a rat in the night when his food ran out. The darkness kept him hid as he left into the streets but he stumbled and cut his skin and tore his clothes into rags. He checked every corpse, satchel, and everything again and again to find food. He used up all of his energy looking for it and was starving. When he thought about hunting birds or leaving it was too late. Standing became too much for him, and the sounds of bombs became just a pounding headache that he learned to ignore. As he lay helplessly on the floor he dreamed of a small boy and his friends trying to climb up short walls to a big garden. Then a man came and said, "Walls were meant to keep animals and children out," before handing them a carrot then telling them to go back home. He saw the two monks preparing food on a huge stone stove. Every family started coming to the kitchen and lined up or knelt at tables. Children waited impatiently as they watched elders go first with a bowl. The men who kept the animals brought eggs and milk to fill pitchers and past out bags of treats to the children and babies. Then the boy passed out at the statues feet.

Days later, the squeals from brakes slowly alerted the unconscious boy. He started to hear people hollering and breaking boards. Then the door of the temple was jarred open and the boy jumped up in fear and ran like a scared cat before falling. He was taken up into the arms of a soldier named Three. As Three washed the boys face and hair to revive him, he became a real mystery. The water revealed a blonde haired, blue eyed boy, in the middle of Korea during the war. Then a voice from outside said, "You find anything Sarge?" and he replied, "No, just a scared cat. You guys go on and leave me a jeep. I'll catch up with you in a couple days. I'm going to bury some of these people." They answered, "Yes, Sir Sarge," then left. Three sat down with the boy next to the fire with rekindled flames from fresh air. He gave the boy water then opened up a can of K rations and set it by the fire. He had a chocolate bar as well and gave to him. While the boy was eating Three asked questions but the boy never spoke a word. When the can of K rations was hot he fed it to the boy while telling him all about himself. He started by saying, "Boy where's my manners, my name's Three, almost three years ago I came here. A few years before that, I was in the Japan war not so far from here. Somehow I figure that war ain't worth it unless you make the most of it. So now I got you and I got to figure out just what to do with you." Three continued his story while thinking of a solution, "My first year here I was in Seoul a lot and I know a lot of women there but that ain't no place for a boy. You see, I figure I need to take a little R&R every now and then to keep my mind on the job ahead. So I frequent a few places and have a few beers and laughs then go back fit, straight minded, and ready to do my job. The facts are most of time when I'm ready for some R&R I tell my Lieutenant, I think I need to do some recon work. That's when I leave to scout out some bars. He really thinks I'm out winning this war. In fact most time I really am. One time I got a little off track on the other side of line up North. I ended up in a card game with the enemy himself. You see they like to spy a little too, while taking a bit of R&R themselves." He kept talking as he fed the boy, "Well, we traded off some stories by betting for them. Most of them were old and some were just false info. Afterwards we left went back to war to fight against each other. Well, I won a story about a beautiful Princess that the monks kept hidden. They say as long as she's alive her country and people will be safe from this war and they can never lose. They wished they could find her so they would win the war, but they knew that monasteries and those monks were off limits. They also said no one wanted gods or those monks against them. She was said to be prettier than any other woman on earth and no man has ever seen her except for the monks. Naturally, I was extremely interested in finding this woman. Anyway when I left that bar I headed straight to the monastery. I was just down the road a piece trying to figure out a way in when the gates opened and a cart pulled by two monks came out with a big monk driving and shouting out orders. Next to him sat the most beautiful woman I have ever seen. Immediately I fell down to the ground face first, rubbing the dirt in my clothes and face. I laid still and played dead hearing the cart approaching then she ordered them to stop in Korean. She told them, I figured, to put me in the back and check on me. While we rode I moaned a little and each time I did she looked back with a smile. After riding most of the day in the cart I fell asleep. When the cart stopped again I woke and watched these monks go to the side of the road and took cut bamboo and tree branches away to reveal a pathway. As soon as they cleared the path we took a trail in a few hundred feet then stopped to replace the cover. They continued down that jungle path for an hour, just before dark, when we came to a clearing with a small hut. She went into the hut and lights came on. Then she came to the porch and told the monks to bring me in. So, they brought me in and laid me on a bed next to the kitchen fireplace. She talked some to the big monk, I couldn't understand anything, but I knew she was sending them on. As she cooked me some food she heated up water for me. Occasionally she turned to look at me with a smile. This had to be the most beautiful woman in the world that the North Koreans were describing as the Princess. Anyway she brought me some food and fed me small bites. I about choked on every one of them. After eating she poured hot water in a tub for me to take a bath. Then she started to unbutton my shirt. Just about then our eyes met and I leaned over to kiss her and she backed off, slapped a wash cloth in my hand, and retired to her own room. Boy, I just blew the best thing in my life and knew that she might never forgive my gesture. As I bathe I heard her praying much like singing a beautiful love song before turning out the light.

"The next morning I woke up to the smell of freshly cooked bread and my uniform was clean hanging from a curtain rod. She sounded like an angel singing from her room. When she finished she came out of her room with her hair finely combed and put up with a gold pin. She wore a beautiful red garment embroidered with gold. Looking at her I knew she was royalty and fit to be a real Queen. I was not worthy of this prize at least not until I cleaned up a few things before attempting to be her King. Not knowing how to say anything in Korean, I spoke in English, 'Ma'am, I'm real sorry about last night and I'm not any kind of gentleman to have taken leads as I did. So If you excuse me I will take leave this morning and I hope you accept my extreme apologies for my actions'." Three continued to talk to the boy until he fell asleep next to the fire. In the morning Three fixed breakfast for the boy before waking him. Once the boy was up and eating Three said, "Boy I have to leave a couple days to find you someone to care for you, I can't keep you myself but I'm hoping I know someone who can. And if she's still there you'll be kept safe. If you're with her, those monks will always protect both of you, and the enemy won't mess with them monks. I'm going to have to leave you now. You have plenty of food and water, and just stay put, next to fire, and don't go out until I come back."

The boy stayed speechless until Three got up to leave then he screamed out, "Don't leave me, please don't leave me." Then Three sat back down and held the boy, trying hard to figure out his next step.

The soldier in Korea feeding the orphaned fawn is trying to figure out his next move. He can't take this little guy with him but he hates thinking of leaving it to starve.

CHAPTER FIVE

BEHIND THE FLAMES

Three sat back down next to boy and placed his arm over his shoulders hugging him close. Then he told the boy another story saying," "One time I was in Seoul, fourdays on a binge, and my unit left me. He made a funny gesture with his face then continued, "They had moved up to the line. After the girls sobered me up I had to figure a way to catch up. I also needed to avoid any encounter with regular forces. I secretly ended up at an Army Air Corps Division and had an old friend hook me up with a pilot to air drop me near my unit. While flying close we encountered the enemy on ridges below and interrupted an ambush. I was desperately seeking an alibi, and now I had the perfect one. During our recognizance flight we fired on the enemy and they returned heavy gunfire which tipped off the enemy's position. When I got back the Lieutenant recommended me for the bronze star and gave me a week's pass R&R back to Seoul." Three, kept telling the stories until the boy again fell asleep.

Leaving the boy with his pack under his head and plenty of food Three drove all night to reach the monastery by early morning. Then he frantically blew his horn and pounded on the gates. Finally the Head Monk came out and Three ask him, "Do you speak English?" The Head Monk replied, "Of course, I'm a graduate of M.I.T. in Boston, Massachusetts in 1931." Three said, "Well Bulla, Bulla, I need to find her, the Princess you know. I have to find her now, because I found a boy in a torn up city up in the mountains near the coast. The boy is a blonde hair blue eyed American from the South I suspect. God, no offense intended, only knows how he got there. And the boy is living in the temple and I need to leave him with the Princess." Then the Head Monk readily replied, "Priestess not Princess. This place in the mountains I need to see it and now! You take me there and I'll get the boy to her." Three said, "No dice I need to see the woman now." Then the monk gathered a few provisions and papers then left with Three alone. They drove two hours to the turn off where they uncovered and covered the path as they had done two years before. When they got to her hut the Priestess was standing on the porch. Three got out, and climbed the steps with his eyes fixed on her and reached out to grab her hand. Then the Head Monk raced up the steps and grabbed Three and she told the monk in Korean it was all right and to leave them alone. Reluctantly, he left them and went around the corner. Then she hugged Three and looked up with a willing look and he kissed her with a passionate kiss. He held the Priestess in his arms a few minutes then took her hand and led her down the stairs. Then he called out, "Bulla, Bulla I need you." The Head Monk then came from around the corner with a fiercely annoyed look, saying, and "Yes master may I help you." "Sure," says Three, "tell her about the boy. I need her to keep him for me." The monk seemingly was translating, but she already knew all about the boy. So did the Head Monk. Afterwards, she rushed back into the hut and retrieved two torches and some transcripts telling the Head Monk that they had to hurry and go to that city. She also warned him to do as she instructed, before bringing her the boy. The Head Monk told Three, "We must go now before it gets too dark." Three asked the Head Monk on the road if he translated everything that he said and explained. The monk assured him that she knew exactly what he wanted her to do.

  While riding in the back seat the Head Monk sat quietly reading transcripts that he wrote years ago. The first transcript read, "The Priestess vision is of a beautiful old city and a mother bathing with her little boy with in temple spa. Then she saw her eating with husband and child in temple dinning room. After that Korean children were playing with the little blonde haired boy in street. Women were sitting next a fountain washing clothes while older men were sitting on the porch playing board games and watching the children play." The comment on the bottom of the transcript read, "This was her first vision when someone had not died." As he skimmed through the transcripts he came to one and read in the opening statement, "The Priestess sees a soldier found the boy who was alone and starving in the temple." Then Three asked the monk while driving, "Bulla, Bulla what's you readin'." The Head Monk replied, "I'ze fixin' to read the story of when we found you face down in the dirt playin' dead." Three said, "Are you making fun of me, what story, that really happened." Then the Head Monk put down the pages and replied, I don't have to make you look funny, you can do that just fine without my help." The Head Monk continued asking Three, "What happened to the boy?" Three answered, " He was alone when I found him. It looked like everyone left him. They missed him somehow. And now, he's waiting for me, in the temple, to get back." The Head Monk said, "Do you expect me to believe the boy's been waiting for you two years and she's been waiting for those same two years as well?"

Three said, "What the hell are you talking about. I found the boy two days ago; he couldn't have survived there more than two weeks. What do you mean she's been waiting for me to come back for two years?" The Head Monk exclaimed, "God knows, she's been waiting for the boy for two years!" Both of them were thoroughly confused and stayed quiet. It had been two years since Three left the Priestess hut the first time. She thought then he was asking her to keep the boy and was leaving to get him, just as they were now. Neither one of them were ever expecting to see each other again, only the boy. The Head Monk had long since forgotten Three until he came back with news of the boy. Now, no one had any idea what was going to happen next. They were headed to get the boy from a hidden city which only existed in stories. The first time the Head Monk had heard of the hidden city, he was very young orphan being raised in the monastery. The story was a myth used in their teachings to warn new monks. It told a story about a small number of radical monks who left the monastery. Those monks sought after a new path and left to build a hidden city. They wanted to live away from the problems of the world in peace. It was said when they left the protection of the monastery, this offended the gods, and those monks were cursed. It was also said that no one ever heard of them again. Because of these monks, all monks were told if they ever spoke against the world or left they would follow in that same curse. Now, he was going to see the hidden city of that myth where the answers lie. Though the Head Monk was a Priest he was a Scientist as well. He believed that all things which that existed without explanation only lacked discovery of some key element of scientific research. He was hoping to find tangible evidence, or at least some sort of logical explanation.

They drove through the night reaching the city by early morning. The Head Monk was amazed by the sum of devastation which over shadowed its magnificence. As they entered through its broken gates the boy ran midway down the stairs then leaped into Three's arms. Three took the boy back into the temple as the Head Monk walked through the city. When he came to the square he tasted the water from the fountain and spit it out, it had become pure oil. Afterwards he went back to the jeep to get the torches then went up to the temple. There he found the boy sitting on the floor in Three's arms next to the fire. He told the boy in Korean, "I need you to do me a favor, and then he asked Three in English, "Please let the boy come with me." Again talking in Korean he told the boy, "Please take the torches and light them from the fire below, and follow me." Afterwards the monk led the boy to city square and started to chant and pray, Three recognized the chant, it was the same song the Priestess sang that he sang as he poured water from the fountain over each body before telling the boy in Korean, "It's time to clean up this mess you made don't you think and put everything back the way it was." Three didn't exactly know how the boy understood Korean or what they were talking about, but knew the boy understood perfectly. The boy had plundered then stole their clothes and presents of food. Three stood bye as the monk bowed his head to the boy, then grabbed the boy's hand with one lit torch and lowered it to the water. The water in the broken fountain caught fire and the flames spread to the oil soaked bodies. As the flames went up the boy gazed into them and he saw each person in the hidden city smiling and laughing. Some were walking in the streets of the city waiving to him. Children were playing and elders playing board games looked up smiling and waiving. His mother sat at the fountain with the other women of city smiling and waiving to him also. Then his father stood across the street in front of the church waving too. There were the two old monks with both of their hands raised as if they were cheerleaders. The Head Monk asked the boy in Korean, "Tell me in Korean what you see." The boy descriptions overwhelmed the Head Monk. He started crying like a baby. Three could only stand there, not wondering how the boy knew Korean or how the water burnt. Or for that matter, he wasn't wondering what the boy is seeing that made him smile so big? But why was this big monk fusing so much? He was sitting there sobbing with had his hands over his eyes. Three sat down beside him and said, "Bulla, Bulla get it together man, you'd think this was your first funeral." Three also sat there with his eyes squint, trying to see something in the flames as well. He started to get the boy several times, but the Head Monk took one hand from over his eyes and stopped him every time he tried. As Three stood back watching this event he knew both of them knew exactly what was going on. But, this phenomenon was bigger than anything he had ever seen before. The boy watched as the monk listened for over eight hours until every corpse was consumed. Afterwards the oil turned into fresh water thus dousing the flames. The boy's countenance bore a smile and his renewed strength made him look invincible. When they returned to the temple Three watched the boy gather up everything he had taken and put it in a pile on the floor. Afterwards the boy told Three, "Please go out with all of your things." When

Three left, the boy lit the pile and walked out of the temple doors backwards, with the entire room filled in flames. The boy said, "We can go now; I'm ready to go home."

Three drove as the boy slept with his head on the monks lap in the back seat. Once they reached the covered pathway the Head Monk told Three, "I'll take him from here." Three replied, "I want to take him in and see her again one last time," but the monk said "No, these are her instructions, please go back to your Army and I will bring the boy to her." He knew the Priestess and monk were right. He'd been away from his unit now four days and it might be a week before he found his way back to them. So Three hugged the boy and kissed him and said, "I be back soon boy you take care of your mama she's my woman too, now say goodbye to your dad." The boy replied "I love dad." When Three left, everyone had tears in their eyes even the Head Monk was balling like a baby again, especially when Three hollered out "Bulla, Bulla you take care of them too," just before driving off.

The Head Monk brought the boy through the jungle to the clearing by early dark. The lights came on in the hut and the Priestess came down the porch and grabbed the boy from the Head Monk's arms. She hugged him tight and kissed him, and the boy felt as if he were in his real mother's arms. She asked the Head Monk to stay if he wanted to until daylight. But the Head Monk said the full moon was out and he had a lot to think about. The boy understood every word and left her arms to hug him, and said you're just like the other two monks in the city, but you cry a lot. Then as he left the boys grip he started blubbering again and left. When the boy entered the house his food and bath were both hot and waiting. It distress her as she helped the boy out of all his torn clothes and seeing all of the scars left by unmanaged wounds. Once they were off she sat him in a hot bath and fed him hot soup while he soaked. She kept going back for more and more soup trying to fill up his empty stomach but ran out. She also ran out of hot water after going back over and over for clean rinse water. The boy had acquire so much dirt, sweat, and blood it was next to impossible to clean him up good in one day, or for that matter so starving, to fill him with one meal.

She knew the boy had been in Korea since he was six years old and now he was almost thirteen years old. She also knew that there was going to be many more days to clean him up, fill him up, and show the boy his destiny. This was a new beginning for both of them. In fact she already had clothes made for him that were just his size. Over the past two years she had been making him night clothes, day clothes, shoes, even some hats, just waiting for this time to come. Once she got him dressed and laid him down. Then kissed him on the forehead and then left into her room. He heard her start praying a beautiful song. But, before she finished it the boy fell fast asleep. The next morning the boy woke up to the smell of fresh baked bread, eggs, and syrup. It was the biggest breakfast he had ever seen, and she brought it over to him on a tray and placed it over his lap, so he could eat in bed. Kissing him on his forehead again she said in Korean "Good morning, my gift of life." And he replied in Korean, "Not yet I'm still to dirty to be good present." She replied, "Perhaps." She watched him eat then led him into her room were the little statue stood with the torches and the base of fire. She asked him, "Did you see into the flames" and the boy answer telling her everything that he saw. Then she said, "I saw you too, please light the torches and follow me." She led him to a courtyard and a pond with a statue with water pouring from its mouth. Then she said, "Please quench the torches into the water" and when he lowered the lit torches to the pond the water caught on fire. They both looked into the flames and saw the hidden city and his parents, friends, the elders, and the two old monks. And she asked, "Who are they and what are their names." The boy stood a moment then answered, "I don't know."

CHAPTER SIX

THE TORCH MASTER

Their vision lasted forty five minutes. Then they sat down on the garden bench next to the pond. She had so many more questions to ask the boy, but he could not answer any of them. Her only hope was to trigger more of his memories. Just the mere resemblance of the Head Monk had the boy remembering the two old monks in the hidden city. This made the Priestess sure, by combining the stories about herself, then reading him the transcripts of her visions; he would regain his entire memory. So she started by telling him her own story. "I grew up in the monastery and don't remember anything before then. My parents left me with the monks as an infant. The Head Monk never learned the reason or he kept it a secret. As a baby I only remember the monks caring for my every need, even the Head Monk. But raising a child, who wanted to run loose in a monastery, had to be very distracting. So the Head Monk gave me the two torches to light lanterns. He told me I was now going be the Torch Master. This job was created to keep me busy and out of trouble. He came up with a long ceremony that included prayers for me to learn. I was told that the fire had to be lit a certain way, as not to offend the gods. For several years I lit the lanterns and perfected my ceremony. The Head Monk noticed how beautiful it had become and asked me to perform it at a cremation. I was about the same age as you when I lit the oil covered body with my torches. It was then I had my first vision in the flames. I could see the decease man standing in meadow, smiling, and waiving. There was a deer jumping over a brook. I told the Head Monk but he did not believe me. He said I was traumatized and never asked me to be part of another funeral.

"Then one day after someone died I was compelled to put the torches out in the pond. The fresh water pouring from the statues mouth had turned into pure oil and it caught fire. I looked into the flames and saw the person who had just died, happily living in a beautiful place.

While I was telling the vision to the Head Monk he was wondering, not about my vision but, why oil was in the water. He told me it would be my job everyday to end my ceremony by quenching the torches in the pond. Whenever someone died, the following morning, oil water poured from the statues mouth. After doing my ceremony and lighting lanterns I then came to the pond. When I touched the water with the burning torches it caught fire and I stood gazing into the flames. The Head Monk rushed and stood behind me, asking what I was seeing. I told him everything in my vision until the fire died down. Then he reached up to the mouth of the statue and tasted it. The water became pure. I continued to try to light the water every day. Again the pond only burned after someone died. The Head Monk recognized the fountains predictability and the morning after some one died he would be standing behind me to listen and write down my vision. Over time his studies led him into keeping accurate records of every vision and water samples. The Head Monk ordered his monks to bring him samples two to three times a day. Each sample had to be tasted. Then its purity was measured before being recorded. He called it scientific research, even when he had the other monks dig around the base of the pond, looking for buried pipes.

"These records of my visions went on for some time before approaching the Head Monk. I told him that I needed to tell my vision to the grieving family. I knew he still didn't believe any of my visions. The Head Monk explained to me that because I was traumatized as a child I developed a fascination over those years as the Torch Master. I was furious, and inquired of him, if I had imagined the fire too. I then insisted by telling him that if he did not do as I asked this may offend the gods, and he might become my next vision. Considering the risk he decided to tell my visions to the family not me. The Head Monk always read the transcripts of my vision to them confidentially. His records always revealed to them some special attribute of their lost love one or the place the family would recognize. Those small details bewildered the Head Monk because this became their assurance and his own written proof.

"My stories of those visions spread throughout the entire country. People came from far and wide with pictures or clothing of love ones, they were enough to make the pond burn. They wanted to see me, but the Head Monk refused. He told them that my visions were given by the gods. He also included that my power could be lost if anyone was allowed to see me. But he never revealed it to me until I left the monastery. Then the Head Monk told me he only said this to protect me. It seemed to him that the all Korea considered me to be the gateway and keeper of eternal life."

She pause her story then asked her new son to join her inside for hot tea and a light meal. Then she started back, "About six years before I left the monastery to come here the police authorities came there to question the Head Monk. They wanted to know if he had given refuge to missionaries or heard about them. The police said that the month before, the Korean military picked up a radio distress call from a plane but the headings of that plane were off the east coast of Japan. It was too unusual that they would have heard this message so clearly they recorded it. Korean officials contacted the American government and they listened to the recording. The Americans research showed this plane was headed to Japan with relief supplies and missionaries from the United States. The missionaries on board were a man, woman, and six year old son. The Americans asked our government to help them investigate. Korean military planes searched our coastline, but never found a plane or wreckage. All police in Seoul were notified to make inquires in every province within the area. They were questioning people, airports, hospitals, and monasteries. The Head Monk told them he did not have them there. Neither did he know anything about them. His only condolence was that he would pray for their well being. A week after the police came with that news, my morning started out the same way. I went ahead and preformed the ceremony and the Head Monk watched from a distance. We were not expecting the pond to catch fire, because no one had died or brought pictures. But when I lowered the torches into the water the pond it burst into flames. The Head Monk ran over and stood behind me asking what I was seeing. Astonished, I told him I was seeing a beautiful old city that was set apart from the rest of the world. I described it as being the greatest and most wonderful place I'd ever seen. Within a gorgeous temple there was a spa. There I saw a woman bathing with little blond haired boy. She was Caucasian woman with beautiful long red hair. Then the woman and child joined her husband in the dinning room. Two old monks fed them. After eating the little boy went with a Korean woman to play with the Korean children. They played in the street while the women were washing clothes in a big fountain. The elders also watched them as they played board games, under the shade of a porch."

The boy interrupted her and told her, "That was me, wasn't it?" and she answered "Yes that was you, and that is your home. Everyone's still there and it is just like it was, except you.

But they see you with me right now, and they're as happy as you are when you see them in the flames."

She continued her story. "I watched you grow up in that city for three years. I also saw a man who I believed he was your father. He wrote from pages in a book called the Bible. I was able to see exactly what he had written for the two old monks to read. The Head Monk kept all his transcripts from my visions for his records. A few months later he wrote words prior to me I telling them to him. It was obvious to me that he knew exactly what to write before I spoke. I accused him of writing his own version, as an attempt to make my vision read as a tale. The Head Monk explained to me that it was just the opposite. He told me at age seventeen he left the monastery to explore the world. He ended up in the United States. There he studied twelve years. While in America he also learned of the Bible and knew it well. He told me that the words he transcribed from papers that your father wrote were exact wordings of the American Bible. He said he recognized many parts and knew exactly what I was going to say next. I told him no it was impossible. The fact was I never have read the Bible before. How would I know the exact wording. I ordered him to bring me all the original transcripts of visions. I also told the Head Monk I needed all the original transcripts every time he created a new one. This allowed me to study these writings called the Bible."

The Priestess asked the boy to wait. Then she left going into her room. A few moments later she came back with a beautiful hand carved chest. Handing the chest to him she said, "For three years your father wrote these pages. They are the finished Bible in Korean. After your father finished writing these pages everyone was baptized. Then the pond only lit when someone had died or brought me their love ones clothes or pictures to me by the Head Monk. I placed those things next to the statue the night before or early in the morning, before lighting lanterns. When I came back to quench the torches the water it burned and I would see the person behind the flames in paradise. But there were other times when the water stayed pure and did not burn. I have to suspect this was someone who failed to please God. Two years went by and thousands of people came to hear my visions but I never saw you or the city again. Then one morning, almost three years later, the pond caught fire. Just like the first time, I was not expecting the water to light. This would also be my first time seeing tragedy in my vision. In the flames I watched bombs exploding far away from the city. I could see the people talking even screaming at times, but my vision would not allow me to hear. Every day I returned to the pond, it caught fire, I was tormented by what I would see. The bombs were getting closer and closer. What could I do? I felt helpless and could only pray for everyone in the city. The following morning my worst vision happened. In the flames of the burning pond I watched the bombs exploding and hitting the walls. All of the women with children ran into the church as your father and mother grabbed babies and helped elders inside. Then a bomb exploded on the church. That vision ended with all the men turning back in slow motion and searched for the bodies of their love ones. Two days the flames revealed the men and the two old monks struggling to find all the bodies and preparing them. Every victim they found was dressed in fine apparel. Wrapped gifts of food were left with them for their journey to the next life. They were all laid side by side around the fountain to be cremated. The bombing started back hit the fountain and broke its walls then the water soaked the ground and the bodies. I watched them try over and over to set fire to the love ones but the water was pure. I know now why the water did not turn to oil. You were left covered underneath the debris. Again the bombing started and everyone had to leave running into the jungle. The bodies were exposed to seagulls, as I watched hundreds of them fly in to pick at the remains. It had been three days after everyone left I saw you in my vision digging your way out of the rubble. I watched you everyday suffering in that city as the bombings continued. I could see you scavenging for food and clothes at night. You were starving before the soldier came. He feed you and talked to you."

The boy interrupted again saying, "That was Three, my dad and he said you his woman and my mom. He said I should take care of you." She hugged him closely and said, "His name is Three? I am your new mother and he may be your father, but I believe he forgot to ask me to marry him." She asked him, "Did he tell you about me?

The boy replied, "He told me you found him aside the road and you brought him here."

"Yes," she said, "He came here one year after I came to this place. The Head Monk built all this for me with the other monks. I thought then the soldier had gone to get you, so I cooked and cleaned. I made a place for you. But he left for two years. I didn't know until the Head Monk drove up with the soldier in that jeep that this vision was just now happening. Then I sent our soldier," she hesitated and said, "Three, with the Head Monk to get you. But first I ran back into the house to get the torches and instructed the Head Monk to have you cremate those bodies so everyone in the city would be set behind the flames in paradise. It was all happening again and I had to prepare for your coming. I too had to wonder too if someone else had the power use the torches and see a vision in the flames. I prayed you would see in the flames. I didn't know until you came here and told me your vision. Now, your destiny as a Torch Master is with me and we will be together for eternity."

CHAPTER SEVEN

M̴ISSIONS OF SORTS

The following morning after breakfast the Priestess again told the boy, "I watched the city being destroyed and you suffering in it for fifteen days. After that I never saw you again and the Head Monk asked me to remember as many details as I could about the soldier coming. He wanted me to describe this house, my kitchen, and anything else I had envisioned. Then the Head Monk left the monastery with six of his monks on a special mission. They left for a month actually coming here to build me this place. The Head Monk had it built it just as I described and added a few touches. This pond with the statue is his small replica of the one at the monastery. I was nineteen years old when I left there to come here. Once a month the Head Monk came to see me and brought me supplies. A year later I decided return with him to visit with the other monks. When I was coming back here from the monastery I found our soldier laying face down in the ground."

The boy then blurted out, "He was just playing dead so he could meet you, and he won you in a card game!"

"Really!" the Priestess replied, "A card game, when our soldier was laying face down in the dirt he was playing dead? But, I knew he was only doing it to stop me, then to bring you to me." She inquired of the boy "But, what card game?"

The Priestess listened and smiled as the boy explained. Three's secret mission literally was dealing with the enemy. Her smile didn't last long as she exclaimed, "Our soldier did not come back! When he left to get you I started cleaning and making a place for you. As days past by I made you clothes and shoes. But he never came back. I made you clothes for months. I went to the fountain every day sometimes four times and a tried to light the pond's water but it would not burn. I was looking for you and the soldier. I thought if he were dead I might see him behind the flames. This would have explained why he could not return. A year went by and I finally wrapped all your clothes and hid them away with the papers. I was even feeling foolish having believed in my own visions. I stopped going to the pond. I secretly hoped it would never burn again. Even the Head Monk stopped coming back to see me. He probably reverted back to his old reasoning. But, this time he could not dismiss my visions as being my imagination. Your father's Bible was written in Korean as proof. His own recordings were also. He still sent me supplies by the other monks. We grew apart over those two years."

She got up with boy and went back inside. Once seated with the boy she said, "Four days ago, our soldier came back with the Head Monk to see if I could care for you. I had given up any hope of ever seeing you or a vision again. Right then I knew exactly what to do and how to do it." She hesitated as tears formed in her eyes she said, "You are with me now, you are real, the hidden city was real, and you're seeing the visions of your city set behind the flames that really exist. I thought I'd never see the Head Monk for a loss for words. Now, he's like me. We can do nothing but cry!"

She got up wiping her tears and went into her room with the boy where there was a huge wooden trunk. She asked him to open it. After she lifted the lid she took out the small wooden chest that held the Korean Bible. The Priestess opened it and asked, "Have you ever read the words your father wrote." The boy said, "I can only remember those two old monks reading papers like these everyday. I also remember him writing those papers." The Priestess asked, "Who was he?"

I don't know I can't remember, you said he was my father. But Three's my father. I need to rest I'm feeling bad." The Priestess was troubled and feeling the boy's pain. She knew that he might never fully understand or recover.

The next day the Priestess led her boy back into her room. She opened a huge wooden trunk and took out the small wooden chest containing his father's. Bible. Underneath it were clothes for him, and thousands of transcripts of her visions. She went through a stack of pages and pulled out a large hand full of them. Then she led him outside to the porch bench where she read a few of her first transcripts before she found this page.

25 Oct. 1945 this is first vision when someone had not died that we know of. The Priestess sees many men bringing a woman and her small boy into a beautiful city. Then she sees an older monk giving the woman a robe and clothes. He is leading her and her boy, through the temple, to a spa. The woman is left to bathe with her small blond haired boy. She got out of the water and put on a white robe and is dressing the boy. They are going into the temple dinning room her husband is waiting. When she entered the dinning room he kissed her and hugged the child. Another old monk is setting food for them. They are eating and talking but it looks like they are whispering. The first monk comes in and talks to the other older monk. Both monks leave. The boy is still eating but the parents are discussing a problem. Now, one monk came back with a woman. She says the monks seem to be asking the mother to let the child go with her. The boy leaves with the Korean woman. That woman took the small boy to play with the other Korean children. The Priestess sees all the women sitting at a big fountain washing cloths, laughing and talking. Elders are watching the children with them while playing board games sitting on the porch in the shade.

The Priestess asked him, "Do you remember anything." The boy said, "That was the first day of when we came to the city. Mom kept bugging me to say kamsahamnida. But, I didn't want to."

The Priestess asked, "Do you remember her name?" He replied, "Only mom. But I think my name is Michael."

Every day they read the pages together and Michael would remember a little more and tell her all their names and stories. He told her about his fathers church and taught her the songs, "I got the joy, joy, joy, down in my heart", and "Jesus loves me this I know". She told Michael, "All the miracles in the Bible are based on people being used. These papers are evidence that God used your missionary father and mother. Now I believe God is using us. So we will wait to see what happens next." Meanwhile, the Head Monk went back to the hidden city for two months, drawing sketches, taking notes, and admiring everything Paul had marveled over six years ago. He wanted to rebuild the city with his monks when the war ended. Finally he returned early one morning to the Priestess hut. To the surprise of the Head Monk Michael was reading a story. Finishing the story the Head Monk told her, "I was wrong and know your visions and Bible stories are not only possible but probable. She invited him to read a page she picked out. He started reading the page about the monks and all the people getting baptized by Michael's father. Then she asked him can you find us a Christian pastor. He told her he only new one place to find one. That entailed finding Three. A big smile came upon her face and Michael's shouted, "Three".

"Yes", said the Head Monk and stated. "Only Three would know were to find someone that important."

The Head Monk returned to the monastery and got five of his monks and the cart. He had them load it with two mattresses, pillows, blankets, food, and water for a long journey. When they left the monastery it was like a horse race. The Head Monk was riding in the driver's seat heading back towards Seoul. Two monks pulled the cart with three monks sleeping or resting in back. Every two hours he woke up the three monks. Then two of the monks sat on the back and ate while the other made hot tea for the Head Monk. After the Head Monk received his tea he sat it on his seat and clapped. The two monks pulling never slowed down. Then the other two monks that were rested sat ready. At the second clap they jumped off the back and ran ahead of the cart. It was a beautiful thing to see as if they were in a relay race, passing the torch. They made the change so smoothly the Head Monk's cup of tea on his never spilled a drop. Meanwhile the other monk inside the cart fixed the Head Monk a happy meal to go and went back to sleep. Two hours later he woke all three sleeping monks again and they made the next change. Except this time the Head Monk was getting ready to switch positions with a new driver. So before giving up the reigns he instructed his relief to fix him a night cap of warm Sake instead of hot tea. The Head Monk didn't set the Sake on the seat though. He turn the hot Sake up and drank it before he clapped and everyone switched places. After all that he went to sleep with the other two worn out pullers.

At mid morning the Head Monk switch places again and drove through the outskirts of Seoul. With the Head Monk driving they were passing every car, truck, or motorcycle. Sometimes in heavy traffic they dodged between them or took the shoulders of the road. Carts were not rare in the country but in the big city it was a real attraction. Especially the way these guys handled a cart. They were Mario Amoretti's of the cart racing. People clapped, laughed, hollered, and swore at times. When someone did swear the Head Monk rose one hand up towards heaven and said, "God forgive them Father for they know not what they say." Then the Head Monk had them turn left towards the red light district and ordered them to slow down to a walk. Once in front of the bars he switched places with a new driver. While disembarking he told him they keep circling the block, while circling his hand in the air, like a lasso. Noticing his monks glancing at girls the Head Monk whistled loudly then hollered to them, "Keep your eyes on the road. Looking at women can blind a man."

When he entered the bar to find Three everyone covered their faces except for the girls. They were teasing him asking him if he was getting to lonely and did him or any of the other monks need their company. He started turning various shades of red, possibly from anger, but more likely it was from embarrassment. Then he saw the American soldiers and walked over to them and bowed. He asked, "Do you know Three?" and one impudent soldier remarked, "No, I know one, two, and four but not three." Then the Head Monk severely agitated with his answer restated, "Three, the American soldier." Then one woman said in Korean, "Three's unit is up North towards Pyongyang." The Head Monk knew this was very far away in North Korea. He asked her, "How long?" She replied, "Three left last week and told everyone that they were going to kick there behinds all the way to Pyongyang." One soldiers there told the Head Monk, "Sir, if he's up North all you have to do is keep your ears open, we're bombing the hell outta North Korea." The Head Monk thanked everyone especially the woman that knew Three. Then he left with a concerned look. Once outside he stopped and whistled loud again and they came around the corner with the cart. When they stopped they all looked up at the sky or covered their eyes, while the Head Monk took over driving.

These monks left Seoul on the highway staying in the right lane. There pace was sincere and incredibly methodical, changing every two hours like clockwork. Seventy two hours later they were still going never stopping or complaining. The sounds of war were heard in the distance and an Army jeep started going around the cart when the Head Monk whistled and beckoned for them to ride beside to talk. Once they were side by side the Head Monk asked, "Do you know Three?" The soldier on the passenger side said, "Three, everyone knows Three, if he's not left his unit on recon, he'd be on the front line. Just keep going towards the noise." The Head Monk thanked him and waived as they went on.

The bombs were getting real loud as the Americans were bombing there way to Kaesong. Army jeeps were flying back and forth and the Head Monk whistled each time one got close to ride beside them. Then he asked about Three. Always the same reply, "Three, everyone knows Three, and if he isn't in a bar, he's up there, just follow the racket."

Finally they came to end of the road blocked by American guards. When they stopped the cart the guard said, "What on earth have we got here? It looks like someone lost their horses. Is this thing even legal?" The Head Monk remarked, "Not only legal but functional and economically sound." The guard replied, "Where did you learn to talk like that? Yale or Princeton?" The Head Monk answered, "Neither one, at Bulla, Bulla U in Boston, Massachusetts." The guard then told the Head Monk "That's it. You're at the line only a few clicks inside the border of North Korea. We can't let you pass because the're shelling the new line pushing our way to Kaesong."

Their encounter with the guards ended with a warning to turn back. So they turned around taking the cart out of sight. Then the Head Monk ordered his monks to pull off the road and stop, as he contemplated his next step. He watched and waited all night and notice when the guards changing every four hours. So, just before daylight at the change of the guards they sneaked up to their station. Then the monks gently hit the soldiers behind the ears with Kung Fu and put pillows under their heads as they fell. Afterwards, they grabbed the cart and continued on their way. When they got to the line the infantry was dug in and quiet, the shelling had ceased about for eight hours ago and these guys were sleeping in the trenches. The monks camouflaged the cart and went to sleep under it while the Head Monk left to visit the soldiers. He stayed out of their sight. Once he was close enough he whispered asking a subliminal question like a ghost. "Where's Three?" The soldier still asleep responded, "Don't know" then he went and spoke with another one saying, "Where's Three" and this took place about fifteen times, until one guy replied, "Who's askin'," and the whisper said "Bulla, Bulla." Then Three jumped up and shouted, "Bulla, Bulla, how's my woman and how's my boy. He said, "The're fine, now the enemy knows too." Three jumped out of the trench and the Head Monk pounced on him to the ground. Three said, "I missed you to, but your hugs a bit over doing it, don't you think," the Head Monk replied, "I trying to keep you in one piece, now keep quiet while I explain!"

CHAPTER EIGHT

TENT REVIVAL

He told Three that he needed to go back to with a Christian pastor. Three exclaimed, "What?!" The Head Monk said again. They heard that too and covered Three's mouth. Then he told Three to come with him to the cart where they could talk. Three mumbled through the Head Monk's fingers "Bulla, Bulla, what cart?" Then he led Three a short ways to the pile of limbs and weeds covering it up. They heard a bunch of snoring coming from underneath branches. The Head Monk started kicking feet and whispered to the sleeping monks in Korean saying, "Are you guys trying to wake the enemy up too? They can hear you guys snoring all the way to Pyongyang." Again Three muttered between the Head Monk's fingers, "What's under that." Bulla, Bulla replied, "You don't need to know everything. Just where can I find a Christian pastor to give the last rights to an old friend?" Alarmed, Three said, "Not my boy," and Bulla, Bulla shook his head no. Three again said "Not my woman," and he shook his head again no. And Three said, "Who then?" and he answered "You, you fool if you don't quiet down and listen!" He continued, "Do you know how to get Christian pastor to come with us? Don't answer, just nod." Three shrugged his shoulders, then the Head Monk said, "I'll take that as a yes." Then the Head Monk let go of Three and flagged him off by fanning his hands backwards whispering, "Seek and ye shall find."

Early that morning Three returned with an Army Chaplain. The Head Monk told Three he must talk to him alone then Three left. The Head Monk told the Chaplain about two American missionaries who came with their small boy and wrote the Bible in Korean. He told them they were killed in a city that was bombed and now they have the Bible, the water, and they have the people who want to be baptized. But there wasn't a Christian pastor to baptize anyone. The Chaplain asked the Head Monk, "Are you familiar with the Bible?" He replied, "Yes" and the Chaplain questioned him and said, "If you knew about Baptism and you read the

Bible you would know that there is but one God. And God sent his Son Jesus Christ as a living sacrifice for us. Jesus Christ is the lamb of God sent to take away the sins of the world. It is written by believing that Jesus Christ is the Son of God that came to this world in flesh then resurrected from the dead we are saved. Further more the Bible states 'His name was above all names and by calling on his name we are saved'."

Then he asked, "Do you believe this" and the Head Monk thought one minute and answered "it must be so, I do". The Chaplain asked the Head Monk. "Now are you ready to be baptized?" The Head Monk answered", "Of coarse, I did not come across the width of Korea in a cart, just to talk about the weather. But you need to come back with me and do this Baptism there." The Chaplain asked, "What makes me qualified to Baptize you" and the Head Monk thought over the question and said, you're a man of God, a pastor, a man who believes and trust in God, you made it your lives work, and you are honored by God with the power given to you to Baptize." And the Chaplain responded, "Are you not a man who believed in peace, love, and respect. Then gave up your life to study and honor those things that were written and told to you from your faith. And now, you know God, He is alive, because he led you to me, halfway across Korea to be Baptized. I could only wish I had that kind of testimony, but God sent me here from my comfortable church to give these soldiers the same opportunity you have and become one of his pawns, to be used and manipulated to win His game." The Head Monk stood speechless with tears in his eyes, and the Chaplain said "Come on let's go find you some water and get you Baptized."

Then the Chaplain hollered for Three, but he was too far away, and the monk whistled loud and Three came running and so did all the sleeping monks. The Chaplain asked Three, "Do you know were there is any water, a pond, river, or stream?" Three exclaimed "The only water around here is at camp showers." "That will do" the Chaplain replied and they all started go. But the Head Monk stopped and asked, "Can you let me have a huddle with my team?" The Chaplin replied, "Take as much time as you need I've got a few things to discuss with God myself."

Then he took his monks aside in a group hug and he talked for two hours explaining the Priestess and her visions, and the missionaries transcribing the Bible, and this was the same Bible he learned when he was going to college years ago. He told them what the Bible said, that there was but one God and he would have no other gods before him. And God was indeed alive and living leading everyone on different pathways for his purposes.

When he finished Three and the Chaplain were waiting and the Head Monk told the Chaplain, "Ask them in English if they believe in Jesus Christ and everything you asked me, and I will translate." And the Chaplain started by asking them to raise their right hand and taking his oath, "I do swear to tell the truth, the whole truth, and nothing but the truth, so help me God. And I have not been coached or forced to say anything against my will." He then continued and asked them if they believed in one God and Jesus was the Son of God by which they might have salvation and everything else that he asked the Head Monk and then he pointed to one at a time for them to respond. And all five said "Yes."

The Chaplain said "Let's go" and they all got into a jeep that Three borrowed and drove right up to the shower tents. There were four showers and two being used. The Army Chaplain went into the first empty shower and stood under the showerhead with a pull chain. The Head Monk followed. Then the Chaplin asked the Head Monk, "By your profession of faith in Jesus Christ who died for the remission of sins. I baptize you in the name of the Father, and of the Son, and of the Holy Ghost." After he pulled the chain that soaked both of them the Head Monk cried like a baby again. Three says, "Bulla, Bulla get it together man your embarrassing yourself in front of these guys." Then the Chaplain stepped out and said, "Now baptize them the same way in your language. And the Head Monk cried like a baby when he pulled the chain over and over again baptizing them in the name of Jesus Christ. Every monks coming out of the shower had his hands raised worshiping, God. Meanwhile Three had seen enough when he was in the hidden city he wanted desperately to become part of whatever was going on between the monk and the boy. Now this, so he asked the Chaplain to baptize him. And the Chaplain said, "Do you believe in one God, and the Son of God Jesus Christ came to this world in the flesh to save you from your sins, and by Jesus' name only can you only be saved?" Then Three replied, "Yes and I always have, and if it weren't for him I wouldn't be here." Then the Chaplain again stepped into the other shower with Three and baptized him. Then four soldiers stood in line and everyone was being baptized. Outside an audience gathered as the tent rocked with the sounds of everyone crying like babies including Three when he came out from the shower.

The next day the Head Monk and Three talked about him coming back to marry the Priestess. Three wanted desperately to come but he had to talk to his Lieutenant. Once Three was at headquarters with the Head Monk he told him, "Let me do all the talking, the Lieutenant doesn't know you know English, so keep your big mouth shut." Three told the Lieutenant that he couldn't lie. He told him he was on to something so big that it might not only stop this war, but end all wars. Three told the Lieutenant he found a secret weapon back the monastery where he left it with these monks for safe keeping. He said, "if the enemy ever got their hands on her…" Then Three hesitated and said "they would win this war." And the Lieutenant said, "Did you say 'her'?" And Three cleared his throat before saying, "A figure of speech like naming your car." He asked Three, "How long will it take you to get 'Her', this secret weapon?" and Three replied, "It depends whether or not you give me a truck to carry 'Her' in, if so I could be back in three weeks." The Lieutenant hollered, "Three weeks, Three, three weeks." And Three replied, maybe four." Well, Three got three days and a big truck. Then the Head Monk had his monks load the cart into it while they rode on back smiling. Every time they hit a bump they all raised their hands and said, "Praise Jesus," in Korean.

CHAPTER NINE

THE HONEYMOON'S OVER

The Head Monk rode up front as Three drove. Three said, "That was the biggest tent revival I've ever seen, when we left that Chaplain was still baptizing, and he probably will be when I get back." Then he asked," What do you think Bulla, Bulla isn't this whole lot better than that cart?" The Head Monk answered, "You could call me Reverend as my monks do now. And what is this? She is now called your secret weapon or was that your car?" And Three grinned and looked at him and said, "And you want me to call you Reverend, hah!" Then the Head Monk asked Three, "How many of these trucks can get like this filled with supplies?" Three said, "What kinda supplies? Food, medical supplies, blankets?"

Three hesitated, and the Head Monk said, "Yes." Then he exclaimed, "Yes!" Three said, "For what? Your monastery, the boy, the Priestess, the people?" Three hesitated again while shaking head up and down then side to side to the Head Monk as he just said "Yes." "What's on your mind?" says Three. The Head Monk replied, "Were going to rebuild the city just the way it was and we looking for a few good men, isn't that your Army slogan?" Three caught on fast and said, "Let me ponder over this deal, meanwhile you just need to remember wedding vows."

The other monks were sitting on back of the truck with the tailgate down hanging feet and kicking them in the wind, like little children. Everyone was laughing and pointing at them, going through Seoul. It was hilarious because the people remembered them a pulling the cart through the busy streets and dodging traffic. Three slowed down like he was going to turn right at the red light district. But, the Head Monk cleared his throat so he stayed straight. Then Three said, "That's right. Keep me on the straight and narrow Reverend and see that I don't go astray."

Six hours later they reached the monastery and the Head Monk told Three that they needed leave the truck monastery and go together by cart. Three hollered, "I only got two more days to get there and back." The Head Monk said, "What do think this truck is going to do when we reach the path? This truck is too wide and will tear into the jungle path, revealing it." Three replied, "Why do you always have an explanation? I wasn't thinking of the path, I just want to get there fast." So they hurried and unloaded the cart, leaving the truck parked just inside of its gates. The trip back seemed to take forever as Three couldn't wait to see them.

Four and half hours later they reached the side of the road and cleared the path. After pulling up and replacing the cover Three said, "This spot is vastly becoming my revolving doorway" and the Head Monk replied, "Vastly, how do you go from outta, ain't, and howdoya to vastly are immense understatements on your use of the English language?" Then Three shut up until they reach the hut.

As they arrived Three heard the boy scream and ran out of the hut. Jumping in Three's arms and Three asked the boy, "Where's your mama?" and he said, "She's coming right now, she's putting on your dress." The Priestess came to the door with her hair up held by the gold pin and wearing his favorite red dress. Three put the boy down and slowly walked over to her and took her by the hand and led her into his arms. They kissed. The Head Monk cleared his throat and said "I remember the vows" and Three said "Let's say them."

Then the Head Monk motioned for the other monks to come, and the boy. When he started to say the vows in Korean she yelled out, "What's going on, where is the Christian pastor?" She continued, "I will not be married without being baptized first! And I defiantly will not marry a man who gambles for women and is not baptized!" The Head Monk smiled and told her to come with him. As they walked to the pond, Three tried to hold her hand but she resisted. She said in Korean to Three, "No, I have to be baptized first!" Then she questioned the Head Monk, "Why did you not bring the pastor?" Three was trying to figure out the conversation and turning to the boy for answers. But she was talking too fast for the boy to even answer and the Head Monk replied to her in Korean, "I am a pastor, I was baptize by the Army pastor, so was Three, and my monks were baptized by me. The Christian pastor gave me his endorsement that God has empowered me to baptize. Now I can baptize you right now." She exclaimed "In this dress, right now?!" and the Head Monk replied, "Why not."

The monk stepped the pond. Then he reached out to help her in. She tried to figure out how to step in but her dress was too long and tight. Then Three said, "Allow me," and he picked her up and placed her over the edge. Then the Head Monk began to baptize her in Korean. Michael started translating his words and Three said, "I know every word by heart and now you have to get baptized and give you a name." The boy replied," I have been baptized and my name is Michael." Three looked at his shirt and pointed to his name O'Connell and said, "See this name on my shirt? You are Michael O'Connell if you want to be and will you please ask your mom and my future bride what her name is?"

Then Michael asked her and she had to ask the Head Monk. He told her name was So Young which meant everlasting beauty. He said he never knew her real parents but they left a card with a flower with her name attached to it, no family name was given. He called her his little Priestess whenever she came to the monastery. As she grew up it seems contrary to him to give her any name other than Priestess.

Three asked, "Bulla, Bulla, I mean Reverend," he continued, "Will you ask So Young if she will marry me? Tell her I'm not the best looking and the most..." then the Reverend stopped him and cover his mouth saying, "I will explain." As the Head Monk asked her and made a few gestures as putting two fingers up over each ear and saying Hee Haw, then another one as if he was grabbing his mouth and pulling it out as to describing a moose, and Three interrupted and said, "I could have said all that myself." Then Three ask Michael, "Will you please ask your mother So Young for me if she will marry me?" Michael asked her and she said in Korean, "Only if you have repented and quit gambling for women."

Michael interpreted and Three picked up Michael then stepped into the pond with everyone else. The Head Monk started by telling Three to raise his right hand. As the Head Monk led the oath Michael interpreted to his mother. "Do you Three O'Connell first repent of your sins and give your solemn oath to stop chasing other women?" Three answered, "I do." Then the Head Monk told Three to put down his hand and he continued the vows, "Do you Three O'Connell take So Young as your wedded wife to love, honor, and cherish, in sickness and in health, for richer or poorer, till death do you part?" then Three said, "I do." Then the Head Monk turned to So Young and asked her in Korean. "Do you Priestess So Young take Three O'Connell as your husband to love, honor, and cherish, for better and worst, for richer or poorer, in sickness and in health, till death do you part?" And So Young said "I do." The Head Monk told Three, "You may now kiss the bride." Afterwards the Head Monk turned to Michael and asked in English, "Do you Michael take this man Three O'Connell as your lawful father for better or for worst, and for richer or poorer, in sickness and in health until death do you part?" Michael answered, "I do." The Head Monk asked Michael in Korean, "Do you Michael take So Young and Three O'Connell as your new mother and father. To love, honor and to cherish, in sickness and in health, for richer or poorer, till death do you part. Then Michael answered in Korean, "I do." The Head Monk said, "By the power vested in me I now can pronounce Three O'Connell married to So Young O'Connell and to their new son Michael O'Connell as a family only God could have put together." Three kissed her again then picked Michael up into his arms and hugged them both. Then the two witnesses raised their hands and said, "Praise God" in Korean.

When they got out of the pond with soaking wet clothes, the water in the pond was fresh. Moments later the Head Monk notices a small oil ring forming on the water and reached up to the statue's mouth. The water turned to pouring oil and the Head Monk exclaimed, "Praise God, we've struck oil!" Then he said, "Michael will you please go and hurry back with the torches so we can dry our clothes?" Michael left and came back running with the two lit torches then lowered them to the water. The oil caught fire and everyone saw the hidden city in the flames and heard voices. Everyone in the city was celebrating and talking. Michael's father and mother said congratulations on their marriage. Then Michael's mother said to him, "I love you, and will miss you but I know you're with your new mother and she's beautiful. Love her as you love me." The Head Monk was talking to the elder monks and asking many questions. They were telling him not try to figure out everything. They said the greatest attribute of God is no one can predict what's going to happen next or the reason. They told him, "Just do what is right and the path will lead you the way God planned it every time." Michael's Father was talking to Three saying, "Thank you for rescuing my son, we know he should have died with us. But God has other plans for him. Now all of you are living for God to do whatever He has in mind." Then Michael started talking to his father and mother behind the flames. Even the two witnesses were talking to the families and children. Three and So Young managed to slip away into the hut for their honeymoon as the flames burnt on for hours.

The next morning the Head Monk fixed breakfast with the help of his two monks. Three and So Young went out to the courtyard and found Michael sleeping on the bench. Three picked him up into his arms and carried to him to their bed in her room. He laid him down and they sat next to them enjoying their new life together as a family. It was hard to believe, as they watched him soundly sleeping, knowing everything he had been through. Then the Head Monk called everyone to eat. Three went in the kitchen and bought back a tray of food for So Young and Michael when he woke up.

Afterwards he joined and the Head Monk outside. Three told the Head Monk, "We have to figure out what to do, I can't stay and it's impossible for me to return without some sort of real secret weapon." Then Head Monk said, "We! I can't figure you out. Every one in Korea knows the amazing Three. You amaze me how you built such a reputation. Something tells me you think of it." Just then Three hollered, "You're right, I know exactly what we're going to do; you just gave me the answer." Then Three said, "We have to leave here. I have to go now. At the end of the month I need everyone to meet me at the monastery with those two torches." The Head Monk was bewildered, and asked Three, "What do you proposed?" and Three's reply, "I proposed once and you made me look like a jackass. You don't need to know. You just need to know how to get it done." The Head Monk just had his words thrown back at him, and he had no idea what Three was planning to do. Then Three asked, "How many people knew about the Princess?" The Head Monk said, "Priestess not Princess" then answered, "Hidden here no one but us." Three exclaimed, "No everywhere."

Michael had woken up and heard their discussion. Then he answered for the Head Monk. "All the people, she told me when she was at the monastery that everyone came to see her to hear her visions. Then they built this place to hide her because she was considered the protector of life." Then Three said, "Great, that's what I heard when I was in a card game with the enemy too. We are going to need more trucks, lots more trucks." Three told the Head Monk, "I need to leave for a while and I will be back at the monastery by the end of the month." He continued, "While I'm gone I need you to find all those people. Tell everyone their Princess is in trouble and needs their help. Tell all of them to head out and go to the monastery with food and provisions to last a month." The Head Monk said, "Priestess, not Princess" Three said, "I going to get a few trucks full of radio equipment too. I will meet you back there by the end of the month."

The Head Monk was beyond being amazed. He was flabbergasted by Three's idea. This was the beginning of something way bigger than anything that happen so far. Then Three told Michael, "I love you son, you stay here and watch out for our woman. Get ready to meet me at the monastery in one month and don't forget those torches." He then told Michael to go tell So Young in Korean what he was doing and what he wanted them to do. The Head Monk sat ready on the cart to carry Three back to get his truck. So Young ran out the house and jumped up into Three's arms. They kissed and hugged each other with Michael. Then Three started to leave and she said, "Stop" in Korean, and Michael said" Stop" in English, and Three said, "Yes, Michael I know. Then she went in packed Three some breakfast in a bowl and handed it to him then kissed him goodbye. Again, they started to leave and So Young hollered, "Stop" in Korean. This time the Head Monk ordered the other two monks to go inside and help her. When the Head Monk called for the two monks they came out of the hut and were eating with their hands full. So Young came out with a bowl for the Head Monk with a pitcher of hot tea. The Head Monk says, "Wait I have a better idea." He told, his two monks to go inside and get all of the food. Next he asked Michael to go get the torches. Once everyone brought everything and loaded the cart they started to leave again. So Young hollered, "Stop" again in Korean. Then she and ran back inside and brought out the small chest with the Bible transcripts. Three said, "I hope this is everything because were running out of room." Michael translated Three's words to So Young and she hollered summoning the two monks to help her as they went back inside with her.

They came back out with the big trunk. Once loaded that cart looked like the hillbillies truck. The Head Monk was in the driver's seat with So Young beside him. Three sat squeezed beside the huge trunk. And Michael rode on top of it. Three told the Head Monk, Bulla, Bulla "I knew you help me figure this out."

While they were headed back to the monastery Three asked, "What do think Bulla, Bulla? you figure out my plan yet?" And the head Monk answered "You go get those trucks, lots of trucks, enough to evacuate Seoul, and I'm going to do some recruiting." Three said, "Yah, that's what I'm talking about." And Michael said, "Yah, that's what were talking about."

So, Three went back to his unit and told his Lieutenant, and he replied "Three, how many trucks? Thirty trucks? Why do you always do everything in threes? Why not three hundred?" and Three replied, "Great idea, Lieutenant. Three hundred and that will really make an impression. We need to have them there before the end of the month." Then the Lieutenant said, "What's happening at the end of month?" Three said, "The monks are moving the secret weapon as we speak in a covert operation." The Lieutenant asked, "Is this secret weapon that dangerous?" Three said, "Our enemies think so. They will try anything to get their hands on 'Her'; and they know how to use 'Her'. If they got 'Her' we will lose this war."

The Lieutenant got on the horn to headquarters better known as HQ and asked to meet with the Field General. Once in the meeting with the General, the Lieutenant briefed him about Three's plans. The General knew all about Three and his reputation. But he also knew Three was no slouch. He knew Three could figure his way out of anything including a war. So he called Three in and asked him, "Three, what was this secret weapon?" Three told the General "I can't tell you either. If you knew, you wouldn't understand, and you wouldn't know how to use 'Her', but the enemy sure knows how to, that's why the monks have kept 'Her' hid for twenty three years." Then the Lieutenant interrupted and said, "'Her' you know like calling your car 'Her'." And the General said "Yah, yah 'Her', and how did you get your hands on 'Her'?"

Then Three explained, "Two years ago, he heard about 'Her' when he was captured by the enemy up North, and he heard them talking about if they could get their hands on 'Her' they could win this war, but the monks had 'Her' hid and safe with them and no one wanted God or gods against them or them monks." Then the General said, "What is she, a religious treasure that they fear?" Then Three said, "General, you catch on quick it's like carrying the Ark of the Covenant." The General said, "The Ark of the Covenant! What's your plan?" Three said, "General you ever play the shell game? If we move the secret weapon with three trucks that might not be enough to fool the enemy. But thirty six empty trucks those are better odds but three hundred would really make this thing work."

The General interrupted and asked, "You said if the enemy got their hands on 'Her' they could win this war. Don't you think it would be a good idea to have troops in those trucks protecting 'Her' if they did find 'Her'?" Three answered, "No sir, if we send empty trucks with drivers only we can't lose because she won't be in a truck. It's only a diversion. So I need a lot of decoys. They will be watching our trucks while the monks will be moving their secret weapon. That's the second part of the plan. As we speak those monks are recruiting everyone to ride in those trucks. Civilians will replace our troops which will further guarantee our success in getting 'Her' here. Because no one knows what the secret weapon looks like and they too will be decoys for 'Her'. The third and last part of the plan General, we need to announce our plans to move 'Her'. We need to let the enemy know and the world know we're bringing 'Her' out of hiding and we're going to end this war with 'Her'. Their only choice would be to try in a short time to find 'Her' or give up before she gets here."

"Are you sure we're talking about a secret weapon or a woman?" Three answered, "Both she is, as I said, the Ark of the Covenant for anyone who has 'Her'. Both sides of Korea respect the fact that she must never be touched and she has to be protected." The General hollered, "By God you'll have your trucks on Friday and a half of a division of fighting men." Three said, "Just drivers sir." The General replied, "Absurd man! You'll get two companies of drivers and a half division." Three said, "No offense intended General but I need those trucks empty to haul civilians, remember? If you put a half division of men in those trucks, all the recruits will be walking beside those trucks. That will look a bit odd. And I need that radio equipment and a few more supplies." The General asked, "Supplies? What kind of supplies? Food, medicine, clothing?" Three replied, "Yes, Sir General. Six thousand civilians have a lot of needs." The General responded, "This thing's getting better and better. I like a good mystery so Lieutenant go get all your three hundred trucks loaded with those supplies, radio equipment and men. You'll be the one responsible for this mission. Tell every man to walk beside the truck and let the civilians ride. You have three weeks no more. And I want that secret weapon moved by our soldiers." Three said, "General sir, when they see our men, this will not be a covert operation anymore." General rebuked Three saying, "Listen you, you're not a one man operation and this is my neck stuck out. A few monks can't protect her." Three said, "General sir, I will need at least thirty of those truck empty to carry the secret weapon and those monks for 'Her' protection. "What?" the General asked, "How many monks are there in South Korea and who can protect 'Her' better than the U.S. Army?"

"God" Three replied, "Remember that Samson slew a thousand men with the jawbone of an ass?" The General replied, "Those monks look harmless but they know that Kung Fu stuff.

You get three companies of drivers, and a half of a division. If you need the trucks empty by God, my men can walk and let those monks ride and civilians ride. Lieutenant, you'll be in charge with your Sergeant. If we pull this off, you'll probably have my job and your Sergeant will become your Major. That is all."

CHAPTER TEN

MAKING HISTORY

On Friday the trucks assembled with six hundred drivers and almost seven thousand men. Three took over as driver of the first truck of the convoy. Riding with him shotgun the Lieutenant opened his door to step out on the running board and hollered, "Let's move out!"

When Three left the monastery over a week ago to get these trucks, the Head Monk with fourteen of his fellow monks had been very busy. All of the monks separated into three groups of five to travel by cart to each province declaring that the Priestess was in trouble and needed their help. They told everyone to go to the monastery with enough food and provisions to last for a month. By the end of the week more than three thousand people surrounded its walls. They came by foot, carts, motorcycles, cars, trucks, or by bicycle. They also came with everything including all kinds of weapons. They brought guns, spears, knives, pitchforks, machetes, and swords. Before Three had even reached Seoul the North Koreans had already heard the news. The news was spreading like wild fire that the Priestess was in trouble and everyone was heading for the monastery.

Korea was always a very strong country that stood together united by beliefs within a system of monasteries. Korea was very serene and undivided until 1592. Then the Japanese invaded Korea on it's East Sea shoreline to start the Injin War. Six years later the Korean's forced the Japanese out of Korea in 1598. In the early 1800's Americans where importing goods and entire Chinese families to America to build railways, cook, clean, make, and launder clothes. They received little rewards but they were able to enjoy the fruits of their own labor. Most came just for the privilege to live in a rich and free country.

However, importing to China by merchant ships took place all through the 1700's by America, Britain, Portugal, France, Spain, and Holland. There were two ways by the Yellow Sea or the East Sea. Either way the ships made stops in Japans with ten sea ports. The Japanese were very receptive but their Emperor's were not. They sent there monks as military led by Samurai to stop every vessel. In the early 1800's they had enough so they formed a coalition. This coalition approach the eighteen year old Meiji who was the next in line to succeed as Emperor of Japan. Usually, this was after the Emperor died or he had to turn over his throne in poor health.

The coalition secretly prepared Meiji for six years to rule with an Iron Fist but to be kind to merchant vessels. Each country agreed to furnish Meiji with warships except the Americans which would supply field armory with rifled weapons. This included guns and rifled cannon that used shell casings for speed and accuracy. Additionally American designed uniforms for the day Meiji would take over the throne. Meiji would not inherit anything until the right time. The warships were the fastest ships known and they were the toughest because the were ex-pirates ships extremely loaded with cannon and gunpowder.

The coalition had Representatives in Congress too that used their power to sway prejudice against the Korean Emperor, Samurai, and monks, but never the Japanese people. The Japanese people always loved trading their goods for foreign goods. But, the Emperor sent his army of trained monks led by Samurai to stop all foreign ships for 100 years.

In 1852 Meiji made his stand using modern rifles to shoot every Samurai and monk then beheading them. Thus, Meiji proclaim to be the Imperial Emperor of Japan. Whereby, his first Imperial order was to open free trade.

Imperial Emperor Meiji warships and new military were actually stronger than all the countries combined. Thus, Imperial Emperor Meiji ordered attacks on countries starting with Korea. The Japanese fleet took every port in South Korea and sailed the Japanese Flagship up the Han River to Hanan the South Korean Capital. Once there Imperial forces shot then beheaded every monk. This all happened in the blink of a eye by foreign warships and his Japanese soldiers wearing new American designed uniforms.

After taking Hanan Imperial Emperor Meiji renamed Hanan to Seoul. Then the Imperial Japanese military were sent all over South Korea to shoot and behead every monk before burning their monasteries. Imperial Emperor Meiji also sent his warships to Russia on the East Sea coastline and conquer the coastline. Imperial Emperor Meiji renamed the East Sea to the Sea of Japan too. This was the primary reason Communism China and Russia tried to create their forces to be stronger than the Japanese.

Then as a humble jester after the coalition created a monster on June 8, 1853 Congress sent Commodore William Perry to Tokyo officially try to ally with Imperial Emperor Meiji of Japan.

In South Korea Emperor Gojong was set in rule of South Korea by Imperial Meiji. Where he would preside from the Deoksugung Palace with his only son Sunjong and his wife and grandchildren. However, upon Emperor Gojong's refusal to accept the killing of monks and policy led to Emperor Gojong and family being held hostage in Deoksugung Palace in the new South Korean Capital of Seoul.

Thankfully, the first Emperor Joseson in 1392 foresight had set aside the best of the best Masters of Kung Fu to the mountains to in Chuncheon monastery in 1414 AD. It was only 46 miles from Hanan and 205 miles from Pyongyang. The monks in Chunchon were the best of the best and day and night to be ready to fight for either Emperor in the case of attack to keep or regain rule. In a sense these monks were any Emperor's wild card to be played when needed.

Thankfully, the Japanese line stayed no further than Seoul leaving Chuncheon Monastery and monks unharmed.

Imperial Emperor Meiji set a tyrannical Japanese Leader too with a Japanese Palace Guard to preside over the Royal Family in Deoksugung Palace. Whereby, he would bring Emperor Gojong with son Sunjong, wife, and children to the Deoksugung porch to been seen with warnings that they would behead their Emperor or the head of one of his family if anyone rebelled.

Despite all this some Koreans still rebelled but were shot and then beheaded. Thus, the saying came up, not to lose your heads. There were no monks or monasteries to go in South Korea. So, South Korean's usually alone sneaked out to bring their deceased to the Chuncheon monastery to be cremated.

From the very first father bringing his beheaded he refused to tell Head Monk Hyun Shik who did this or why. He was fear-full the monks would respond by attacking the Japanese with guns and be shot then beheaded. Our they would be followed to be shot and beheaded. The Chuncheon monks nor had ever seen any weapon other than a bow and arrow or sword. Which were no match for modern guns.

Before the Civil War started in 1861 W.B. Preston was just a merchant ship owner of many vessels all over the world. His favorite ship brought imports from Hong Kong straight to New York and reloaded with American made goods from New York to Florida to return to Hong Kong. Preston knew all about Shanghai and American slave ships at sea he called them as passing by loaded with trade goods straight to Hong Kong. Preston made his trips by sailing around the Horn of South America. It was a dangerous but profitable journey that Preston made many times. But, when the Civil War started in 1861 his journeys by Southern ports were stopped and threatened by the Confederacy. Preston knew the Americans furnished modern weapons even uniforms to the Japanese since 1852. So, Preston made a packed to allow him to continue importing to New York unharmed by bringing a few things like uniforms, blankets, tents, to the Confederacy as he worked as a double agent.

Just before the Civil War ended in 1865 Preston took the opportunity to trade his merchant sailing ship in trade for a military union steamer and gunship, named the USS General Sherman. Leaving New York in his new tin clad and ocean going side wheeled steamer. Preston was anxious try to speed up his journey to Hong Kong. But, he had pass Southern ports first. He was weary as he made ready to pass Norfolk when noticed there were no cannon. So, he entered the Port. It was a fortunate surprise for the Confederate Lieutenant as he saw Preston on the bow of a Union gunship. It was as much of a surprise for Preston not being shot at. Then the Lieutenant told Preston he had orders to stop the first vessel that came and load it with a stockpile of the newest Confederate repeating rifles, Gatling guns, cannons, gunpowder, and shelled ammunition to be sunk out at sea. Instead the Union army hands as General Lee was about to surrender in Appomattox Virginia.

To no surprise Preston did not sink any weapons as he steamed past burned ports in Wilmington, Charleston, Savannah, even Jacksonville, Florida without incident, too. But it was also an unfortunate surprise to Preston that his steamship saved very little time while carrying weapons on a ticking bomb. Despite, everything the USS General Sherman Preston made it around Cape Horn to Hong Kong.

In Hong Kong Preston planned to offer his weapons to Emperor Joseson knowing the Union sent what was then modern weapons and uniforms twelve years earlier. Now he had Gatling guns and repeating rifles that the Japanese finally didn't. So, Preston sent word by Chinese messenger to Emperor Joseson in Korea he had a gift which was a load of modern weapons, cannon , and gunpowder, Gatling guns, and repeating rifles to fight the Japanese.

Preston too had other ships under his the name with American Shipping Company written on their sides. The USS General Sherman was not any good to him neither were the load of explosives. When Emperor Joseson received the message he sent Reverend Thomas Brown his American translator, personal advisor, missionary, and friend for fourteen years.

After Reverend Brown met up with Preston a month later he steamed to Gangwha Straight June 10, 1865 with the two Chinese junks following Preston's vessel.

Then Korean Officials shot across the bow the USS General Sherman. Two Korean Authorities with the three Korean soldier rowed their boat along side of Preston's vessel.

Reverend Brown they told them came baring gifts for Emperor Joseson. The Head Officer insisted they comeon board. As Reverend Brown was explaining to the Korean Authority the soldiers went searching below. Also. the second Korean Officer uncovered the ships forward cannon. Simultaneously, a Korean soldier below hollered, " they are caring weapons," Preston nodded to the Captain as he shot both officers.

Those shots alerted his crew below to jump and kill the soldiers with knives. Their shots alerted both Captain's of junks to attack the Garrison's, as the Guards a mile away heard shots the shots of repeating rifle against muskets and rode fast on horseback to see the end of a massacre.

Reverend Brown was furious but Preston called it an unfortunate lack of communication. Preston blamed the Reverend as this was a gift and he did not send word to Korean's Officials he was coming. Preston also said his cargo was no longer a gift and he was not taking any more chances with a ship load full of explosives. If attacked he will use whatever against any Korean before he gets he to Pyongyang where the Emperor will pay dearly for not informing them he was coming.

Preston proceeded up the Taedong River as the two junks followed. Until they reached the small outposts a mile away. The two officers who were on horseback in a boat waving a white flag. The head officer hollered to Reverend Brown in Korea, "the Taedong River is mined to Pyongyang, you will never make it."

Reverend Brown interpreted that to Preston. Then Reverend Brown asked Preston to go with them back to Emperor Joseson to explain everything. Preston told Reverend Brown to have the Officer come onboard alone in exchange for him and to show him where the mines are. As another precaution Preston told Reverend Brown to tell the Chinese to go before him in their junks.

Reverend told the Chinese to got ahead. They were not informed that the river was mined. So. Preston ship slowly steamed or understanding the exchange Preston steamed slow and carefully upstream. As Reverend Brown and the Korean Lieutenant rode fast and hard to Pyongyang.

When Reverend Brown reached Emperor Joseson with his report. Emperor Joseson sent his palace monks by way of their hand pulled carts and Reverend Brown on his horse back to the TaedongRiver. Once there the monks split up on both banks of he Twaedong with seven monk archers and seven sworded monks. Then they followed the Twaedong down stream. They reached the blast crater in the Taedong where the USS General Sherman exploded and fragments covered the bank.

So the monks hurried downstream until to catch up with the escaping Chinese junks. Then the monks ran to ahead to take aim their arrows on each side of the river.

When the Chinese junks reached the monks Reverend shouted from his horse in the water but on the bank, " What happened to Preston's ships?" One Captain responded, " we did not want to go after Presto ordered us to go in front. We not know the river was mined but knew something was wrong. Reverend Brown said, " if that's true why did you have to go. You out numbered Preston and the authorities. It is because you always planned to steal his cargo." The other Captain started to pull up his gun to shoot and the monks massacred all of the Chinese then set there junks on fire by flaming arrows.

Reverend Thomas made his report back to Emperor Joseson before he went Shanghai to get his report to Congress. His report stated W.B. Preston was a noble man and went out of his way. Unfortunately, neither he or Emperor had time to tell anyone of his cargo.

Abraham Lincoln knew about the Representatives in that were in the coalition and the dealings with Emperor Meiji. Beside Abraham considering the Chinese being brought to Seattle, San Francisco, Portland slaves and the coalition Abraham Lincoln the most unpopular President ever and a Target. When Lincoln gave his Gettysburg Address he said, all men and created equal. So, our Civil War was not entirely about the the black slave trade but the slave trade coming out of Shanghai as well. Abraham Lincoln also found replaced those in Congress. Whereby, /Thereby, the new Congress sent in in 1871 at fleet of five American Warships in 1871 to attack the forts on the Han, Nakdong, and Geum Rivers. Destroying over half of Emperor Meiji fleet.

Kwan Lee left the monastery right after a father brought his. beheaded son to be cremated. Kwan Lee followed him from a distance to Seoul. Kwan Lee had never been to Hanan or it's Seoul. But, he was surprised by a man upon reaching Seoul to hide and go back where he came from. He said your lucky now the Americans are attacking and most of the Japanese are gone to fight the Americans.

Kwan Lee went back to the monastery and told Head Monk Hyun Shik and the other monks the Americans are attacking and Japanese were the name for Koreans fighting back. He debated we need to go help the Japanese fight these Americans. Head Monk and Grand Master said, No we are the best of the best Martial Artist of Kung Fu but we cannot fight for the people only the Emperor's if the people fail we will fight to save our Emperor. Until then we train harder and wait. It is good to hear they are fighting maybe these beheading will stop."

With that said, Hyun Shik put and end to Kwan Lee debates although Kwan Lee still held meetings to build a city hidden away from all wars. Where the people would never know of them and they won't have to protect them only watch over them.

In less then a year, in 1872, Kwan Lee gain nine followers to leave the monastery to find a safe location to build a hidden city. Kwan Lee left two adolescents monks who wanted to go behind. Woo jin was a seventeen year old monk and Eunji who postulant was barely fifteen.

Head Monk Grand Master Hyun Shik learned the true and full story of the beheaded bodies, the Imperial Japanese Invasion, and the Americans role in 1931 from Grand Master Dae Hyun Korean after he graduated M.I.T. Boston, in Massachusetts and returned to the Chuncheon Monastery. Just before he died whereby now Head Monk Grand Mater Dae Hyun preformed he cremation August 15, 1931. Then a month later on September, 12, 1931 a Head Monk Dae Hyun answers a ringing bell to the monastery gates. So Young was left at the monastery as a smiling seven month old orphan baby girl. Under her blanket She had a silken note pinned to dress with her name So Young and a flower embroidered as the meaning was beautiful flower. However, Head Monk Dae Hyun chose to name her Priestess. When his little Priestess became a nuisance at five years old she became his Torch Master. Then as a twelve year old in girl she had her first vision of a deceased love one in front of the family. From that first vision to news spread to all Koreans. Thousands came over the following years with bodies, pictures, clothes, that were enough for her to see the deceased living in paradise or not. Then in late November in 1945 the Priestess had her first vision of the missionaries coming to the hidden city.

When the United States defeated the Japanese in 1945 South Korea became a free country. Monks and monasteries came back quickly but the Seoul line was still South Koreas line for South Korea. This is when a war started between South Korea and North Korea. The North Korean leader Kim II fought as a Communist Leader with the support of Communist China as a guerrilla fighter for thirty years to hold the Japanese from gain any more territory. But, North Korea to was a Communist Country back by China. Communist were not free other than being able to go to the monasteries. But. the United States was willing to fight for Korea to have a free government where the people could elect their leaders and vote. So immediately the United States started talks with Kim II. This was the starting of the Korean War officially start June 25, 1950. Then the push from Seoul to Kaesong began.

Kaesong was the first Capital of Ko Pyongyang by the Japanese. Even today the Korean War exist but there is no fighting. The United States and North Korea compromised on a DMZ acronym meaning Demilitarized Zone. The DMZ dividing line was 2.5 miles wide and stretched 260 miles across the middle of Korea at the 38th Parallel.rea before Pyongyang. It was also the home of Emperor Joseson but he was forced to Pyongyang by the Japanese. Even today the Korean War exist but there is no fighting. The United States and North Korea compromised on a DMZ acronym meaning Demilitarized Zone. The DMZ dividing line was 2.5 miles wide and stretched 260 miles across the middle of Korea at the 38th Parallel.

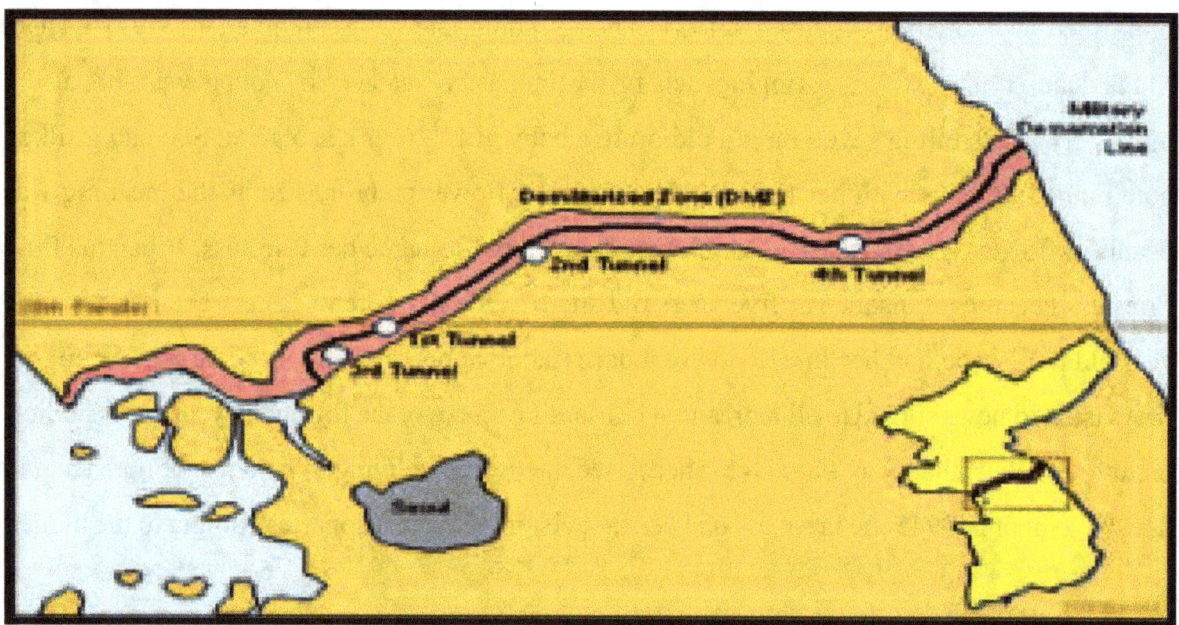

Though Kim II had China's support he always left every monk and monastery of limits to the North Korean army or to interfere with anyone going to a monastery. They could be South Korean, North Korean, or Chinese. This allowed anyone to come monasteries to pray of have some cremated. Thus, monasteries secretly became a way to communicate with people. But, it was the Priestess all Korean's came to see. Kim I1 never learned of the Priestess until the Head Monk and his monks were announcing to all South Korea their Priestess is danger and needs their help.

Also, head to the Chuncheon Monastery with food and provision to last a month. At the same time intercepting the General is send three truck loaded with seven thousand soldier and six hundred driver to bring fetch a Secret Weapon.

Besidesthe Generalmessagessendingtrucksandthousands of troops to get a Secret Weapon every radio station was on location also live TV, every phone was ringing throughout all Korea. In the North Korean headquarters and the Generals headquarters had interpreters intercepting call or making call, radios in Korea, English, and Chinese. As everyone was watchingTV was listening and transmitting every second another bit of real news as it was happening.

Everybody but the Generals could not distinguish 'HER' or 'She' from 'Priestess'. the General was laughing. Many of the leaders disagreed with his policies of Kim11 for monasteries to be off limits. They also wanted go to every monastery and interrogate monks or to assassinate the Priestess. Kim II put a stop to those discussions immediately. He announced publicly, "Any attempt that was made on the monks or Priestess would be treated as a traitor ask it makes him into a traitor to all Korea." He knew any attempt to would also unite all Koreans to rebel against him.

But his military leaders were also very rebellious and they knew how to work around Kim II. They sent spies to every town in North Korea and bribe the people to tell them anything. Whenever they did learn something it was always a great story about a vision given to them by a family member or friend. Their leaders could hear the love and compassion for her in their voices. Every story ended the same way. They considered the Priestess the protector of life with the gods and monks protecting her. They learned too as long as she lived Korea would never lose the war.

They were getting nowhere questioning people so despite Kim 11 announcement leaders blatantly transmitted orders to summons every Head Monk from each monastery in North Korea to come to Pyongyang immediately. They needed to find out just how loyal they would be to aid Communism or the Priestess or if her values were loyal to North Korea.

At the General's headquarter called HQ, as the General intercepted everything the General was keeping track of this as if it were a voting ballot at his own general election. He knew North Korea was chaotic. Also, their leaders were calling for monks and for anyone who knew anything about the Priestess as more and more North Koreans defected.

The General had caught on fast to the Priestess was 'Her' and 'She' was truly their Ark of the Covenant. She was a real Priestess and he heard them say over and over that she is considered the protector of life by all Koreans. The General got so excited just listening to their interactions; he ordered two more divisions to get ready to head out. He knew his orders would be intercepted as well just adding to their chaos.

It was no rumor over half of Korea was heading or already at the monastery. Three also heard the General orders to send two more divisions. He could wonder what Bulla, Bulla was doing. Neither Three or Lieutenant spoke or understood Korean so they hadn't been listening to Korean radio but they were seeing everyone in Seoul heading to the monastery. When Three reached the red light district in Seoul all of his girls were waiting with the rest of the city.

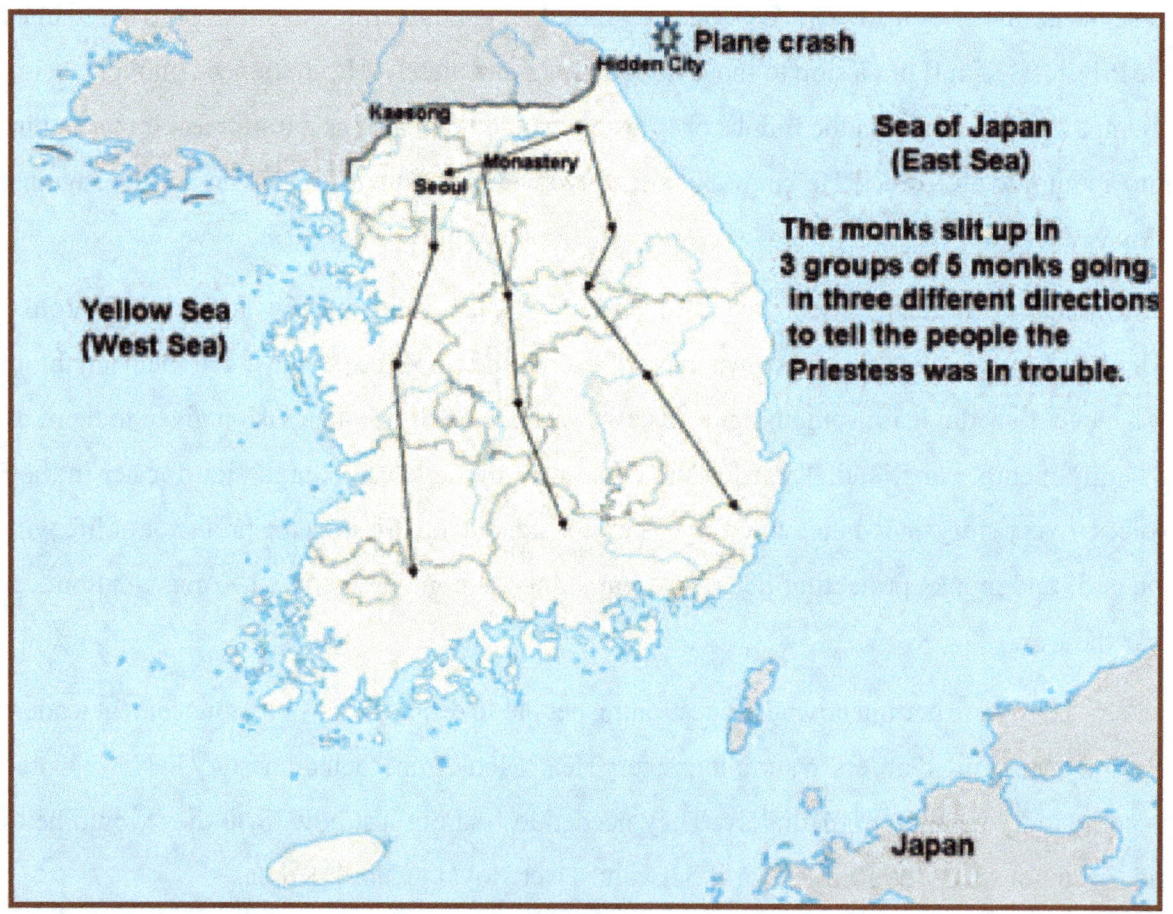

Three reminded the Lieutenant of the General's orders to stop and have the soldiers walk and let the civilians ride. Three also made a suggestion to the Lieutenant asking, "Sir, if the girls rode with us up front in the first truck they wouldn't be able to bother the men behind us." The Lieutenant replied, "Bother the men, tell them not to bother me. I'm married and have my reputation to uphold."

The Lieutenant allowed the girls to get in the back of his truck then gave the orders to get out and fill the empty trucks with civilians. As they drove through the crowded streets the soldiers kept loading them in. Their orders were to allow elders, women, and children to ride first. They traveled at a snail's pace in the biggest traffic jam the world had ever seen. Civilian men walked beside the trucks and often stood on to the running boards. This took place until all three hundred trucks were overfilled with civilians and equipment. Then the Lieutenant order by radio all troop step aside and then fall in behind the convoy trucks. Now there was a single line of three hundred trucks with 7000 soldiers marching behind them being filmed by civilian and military helicopters.

After two days of plowing through crowds, Three noticed a small red pickup truck. The driver was a small Korean man blowing his horn like crazy. He was alone and his truck bed empty. Three said, "Lieutenant, I got to get out and go ahead. You need to just stay on the road; it's about thirty more miles to the monastery." Then Three went and jumped in back of the truck with his girls. He took a minute to explain before one girl jumped out of the Army truck and ran over to the small pickup. She got in the front seat with the frantic Korean driver. Two minutes after she signaled for Three and the rest of the girls. The other girls jumped on back of the small truck as Three squeezed her in the middle of front seat as he rode shotgun. The girls on back announced in Korean, "Let this soldier through he has an urgent message from the General of the U.S. Army for the Priestess. The Priestess is in grave danger and the Army is coming to help her. Please allow us to get through."

They kept screaming the message over and over. Everyone was getting out of the way and the Korean driver was smiling and waiving as he drove. Somehow a TV news truck broadcasting had closeup of the girl, Three, and the driver as they broadcasted live on TV. Three was making the headlines in that small red pickup. Once close enough to see the monasteries they urged Three to run on. Three started out running with four girls just ahead of him yelling the announcement. But Three was out of shape and the first to start slowing down. A Korean man gave Three his bicycle with a horn. Three got had one of his girls on back of it to shout the message as he blew the bicycles horn. Finally Three reached the gates of the monastery.

Monks were already waiting to open them. The General was keeping track of it too as he listen and watched Korean radio and TV broadcast. As soon as Three reached those gates the General and more than half of Korea went wild with cheers and clapping as if he won the Kentucky Derby.

Once inside the gates they closed behind them, the Head Monk starred at the girl on back of the bicycle then asked Three, "Have you already forgotten So Young?" Three replied, "She's just my announcer. Who else could I get that understands me?" Then Three exclaimed, "Bulla, Bulla take me to my woman and son. While we're going explain to me how half of Koreas outside this monastery gates." The Head Monk replied, "Einstein, half of Korea has been always been outside of these gates."

The Head Monk then asked, "Did you get us any trucks?" Three said, "You asked me for thirty truck got you three hundred. And I got sixty drivers in each of them. Ten of them filled with broadcasting equipment, two hundred and ninety of those trucks are over loaded with thirty civilians, and seven thousand soldiers behind them.. Also, the General sending nine thousand soldiers more."

While walking Three to the temple the Head Monk did some math and shouted to Three, "Forget the trucks by my calculations I have over three hundred thousand coming too. How many more, nine thousand." Three replied, "I told you I seven thousand behind those trucks the General more, that's…" The Head Monk said, "A lot, it most probably is half of Korea."

When Three reached So Young and Michael he immediately kissed her and then picked Michael Up and said, "We did it just like we said." Then Three told Michael, "Tell your mama she has over one third of a million people out there wanting to hear her message and bringing enough equipment to broadcast her message around the world." Then he said to the Head Monk, "Now Bulla, Bulla what's she going to say to the world?"

The Head Monk replied, "It's simple, God has sent her a vision with a message. God is coming to stop this fighting. Exchange your weapons for trumpets to announce God is coming to the world. He is coming to end this war and all wars. Anyone who continues to fight will be destroyed."

Three said, "Wow, are you serious?" The Head Monk exclaimed, "Is this not serious?! You opened your big mouth again. Do you now propose to put your foot into it?"

Michael interpreted every word of their conversation until So Young hollers "Stop" in Korean. And Michael said, "Stop" in English, then Three said, "Yes, Michael I know."

Like school children they all sat up and paid attention. So Young said, "Both of you can not tell me what you want me to say or not say. I will tell my people the truth. They will see me and I will give my message anyway it can be done. But, no one will advise me. I was given this power for a reason. This is not about me it is about God. He wants all us to pay attention. God has used every one of us. Not to mention Michaels family and everyone in the hidden city. He has given us a plan and we must do whatever comes next. I will tell your message being already spoken. Only God could have brought about this discussion. I will also say God has instructed everyone to put down their weapons and build horns. Then I will tell them the truth about how all this all came about. They will hear the truth from my words and God's words of the Korean Bible Michaels father wrote."

That night Michael, Three and So Young were in the temple with four monks guarding the doors. The Head Monk waited outside for the first truck. When it finally showed up at dark. The Head Monk greeted the Lieutenant saying, "You must be a General by now. Three's told me he's being promoted to be a. . ." The Lieutenant was surprised and interrupted, "You speak English! So you know I need to see the secret weapon, now where is Three?" The Head Monk and Lieutenant entered to building and approached the guarded doors. Then the Head Monk clapped before his guards stepped aside. When they came in the Temple. Three was lying down with his head in the Priestess lap and Michael was hopping on his belly. Three said, "Lieutenant I would like you to meet my family. This is So Young my wife, and Michael my son." The Lieutenant greeted them saying," I'm very pleased to meet you Mrs. O'Connell and Michael, but Three we need to talk about 'Her' right now." Three said, "Her sir, here 'She' is, this is 'Her' our secret weapon." The Lieutenant hollered, "Three! What about 'Her'?" Three reiterated, "This is 'Her'!" baffled the Lieutenant hollered again, "Three, but she's a woman not a car, and she's not a weapon, she's your wife!" Then Three told him, "Take a seat sir, this is going to take all night I'm sure. So lie down and get comfortable by the fire, Michael can tell you more about her and everything first."

Three and So Young slipped out and spent the entire night together in her room at the monasteryThree knew Michael would tell the Lieutenant everything including the stories of how Three found her by gambling with the enemy and the episode of tipping off the enemy after being AWOL. The Lieutenant was amazed with eyes wide awake at first. But Michael kept telling the stories all night even when the Lieutenant started nodding off. While Michael spent the night telling his stories.

CHAPTER ELEVEN

THE PLAN

The next day the Head Monk knocked and entered the temple. He bowed to the Lieutenant and Michael then scratched his head. The Head Monk said, "Where's the Priestess and Three?" He thought a moment and remarked, "Never mind," and asked if they would like breakfast. After both of them agreed he clapped and six monks entered. Four of them had wash basins and two had towels. The Head Monk said, "Please get washed up before we go to eat." Then he ordered the three monks to follow him. He led them to So Young's room and knocked. Three answered, "Give us a second to put on some clothes." The Head Monk immediately blushed then told his monks to wait for them to open the door. He left them and went to the dinning room. Thirty minutes later everyone met for breakfast. The Head Monk requested Three to say the blessing and possibly repent. Three replied, "No I believe the Lieutenant is the highest authority he should have the honors." The Head Monk was flustered at Three's lack of respect for him. With his sense of monarchy he replied, "Of course where my manners," as he nodded his head at the Lieutenant. The Lieutenant hesitated and Three said, "No Reverend you have the most authority in regards for asking the blessing for which we are about to receive." And the Head Monk replied, "Amen, and thank you Three for blessing our food we are about to enjoy." The Head Monk said, "Please sir accept my apologies for not giving a proper blessing." Then the Lieutenant said, "You're right we need to open with a proper prayer. Dear God, I really don't know what to say, I'm not sure how I fit in to all of this, but the U.S. Army and my General are counting everyone here and especially You for a miracle. I pray Lord for this food which we are about to receive and Your Divine intervention, Amen."

Then the monks served the food. During breakfast the Head Monk said to the Priestess, "Please, allow us to discuss our plans in English while we eat, and Michael please interpret what we discuss to your mother." She bowed and the Head Monk began, "I have told everyone to come here because the Priestess is in danger. All of them that know her powers, to see their families sent to paradise under her protection, have come to support her. The Priestess has seen many visions and every Korean out there including me believe in them." He continued, "Do you know the story of the Second Coming in the Bible? This story is no different. John received a revelation on the Isle of Patmos. The Priestess has seen visions which are true and we have the transcripts read to the families and the Korean Bible written by Michael's father to prove it. She shall convince everyone that there is but one God and He has revealed His will to her by vision and circumstance. The Priestess will tell everyone over the radio and loud speakers in her own words those circumstances. She will also tell of the words of the Bible that came through her. After this she will tell everyone, her people, the enemy, and even the U.S. Army to lay down their weapons and stop this war. She will include God's instructions. Everyone is to exchange their weapons for trumpets to sound God's coming. And everyone who continues to fight will be destroyed. She will tell them this is God's war now and He has had enough. She will broadcast three days then on the fourth day she will make one final broadcast to order everyone to sound the trumpets and every four hours after that as if it were the rapture. The rapture if you don't understand is the calling of God's people. Then we will head for Kaesong."

Three was astounded at Bulla, Bullas plans and the Lieutenant was upset. He said, "You can't expect the U.S. Army to put down their weapons in this war". The Head Monk replied, "You need to pay more attention to the boy's stories rather than falling asleep. I was once a skeptic who could not believe in her visions, miracles, or the power of God. Hopefully, you want to listen more closely to those stories. I have kept records for seven years and have three thousand pages of written testimony that these visions are real and the Bible written in Korean. Her message is the truth; even the U.S. Army is no challenge for God if it has determined that they will keep fighting. I will again encourage you to listen to the boy's stories. I will translate my records if you need more proof. But those records are more than three thousand pages, and there are more than three hundred thousand people out there that are united for one reason. They all believe in her powers and by the time we reach Kaesong there will be seven times more."

"Seven times three hundred thousand that will be over two million!", exclaimed the Lieutenant. The Head Monk ended his words with, "This is the going the biggest event since Noah's Arc and I don't intend to swim this time." The Head Monk added, "I pray you are wise man, now please excuse me as I need to talk to the Priestess."

As the Head Monk explained his intentions she nodded her head as to acknowledge her favorability.

Three and the Lieutenant asked Michael to start telling them the whole story from as far back as he could remember. And over the course of the day they listened intently without interruption or nodding off.

That evening over supper they agreed to set up all the communication equipment the next day for the Priestess to declare her story and message. The Lieutenant called up HQ headquarters to speak to the General. Then he said, "General, do you believe in God and His written word?" The General replied, "Of course I read the Bible everyday just like General Patton and every officer in the U.S. Army should." The Lieutenant hesitated and said," Yes sir, my favorite book."

"And what's the Bible got to do with this call?" the General asked. The Lieutenant started by asking him if he knew about the rapture, and to expect over a million people in Kaesong soon from all over Korea, including North Koreans. Then the he asked the General, "If it's all right General, can my sergeant Three explain his secret weapon?" And Three told the General, "General we are going to setup our broadcasting to reach the entire world tomorrow. Then our Ark of the Covenant will explain everything for the next three days. After that we will be headed to Kaesong and be there before the month's out." The General said, "You got two and half divisions of my men and I need you to make this thing happen or else we'll both be in doing KP the rest of our careers as buck privates." Three replied, "Yes sir, you can count on me and please don't send anymore divisions but you can send us some more K rations and food for these civilians and soldiers, and maybe..." Three stopped as was about to ask for horns and Bibles. Asking for them might be a bit to hard to explain so Three ended his communication with "and thank you, sir." The General answered, "You got it, it will be there in three days." Three answered, "Good number General." before being dismissed.

Before broadcasting the next day the Head Monk wanted the Priestess to write her speech and rehearsed it. She was condescending as if she were scolding him for not believing her from the beginning. He couldn't do anything but hold his head down as she declared her people must not doubt her visions or her message. She said science and humans want to believe only the reality of physical things. But faith comes by hearing and not seeing, and she was being used by God to stop this war and everyone from fighting. She told him that just as those monks built the hidden city from wars so should the world live, not living in greed but as servants to each other and building a society that will never know violence. Then she said, "I'm not afraid to die neither is my son because I have seen the other side, with everyone's family behind the flames."

She continued, "To be absent in this world means to be with God in paradise." The Head Monk marveled at her words as her knowledge of the Bible was beyond his. She brought the words of God into reality as they were being spoken by Him. Then she instructed him to bring her all of the letters and records of her visions.

CHAPTER TWELVE

THE BIBLE

That morning the Army specialist started early setting up all the equipment and loud speakers for everyone to hear her message and broadcast it to the world.

When everything was ready the Priestess spoke to Korea, "My people you known from my childhood I have seen your lost love ones living in paradise after they were placed behind the flames. I saw all of your lost children, parents, elders, and families all living together happily in their own paradise. By coming this shows your belief in my visions and your faith in them without proof. But I will tell you I have all of the evidence that my visions are real. I have thousands of pages of transcript recording every detail that I saw in those visions of your lost love ones. In the next three days you will hear many of your transcripts. You will also hear about my visions of my new son and husband. Both of them came to me the by way visions. I have a book called the Bible which the Head Monk recorded every page from visions. Each and every one of those pages that came through me had the exact wording of a book named the Bible. This Bible is also called the word of God. Not gods but one God. It expresses from the beginning there was one God. For myself there is enough written proof here and knowing my life not to believe any other way. My belief is no other god or gods can exist. I was taught to believe that all life was under the control of many gods. But this God is specific to say He is the only God and we are not to worship or believe in any other God. With me right now are my visions of your families, the pages of the Bible written in Korean, my vision of a boy who should have died, and a soldier that found him. Only the true God could have brought this day and made all these things happen. Transcripts of my visions were written by of the Head Monk. He recorded every word as I told it to him while standing behind me. They are not his words but my words as I watched into the flames and explained what I was seeing. Hopefully from them you will understand and have the knowledge to accept the choices that God has brought before us. He has made all this happen for a reason. God has given me instructions to tell every one of you to lay down your weapons and build horns to announce His coming. This means the North Korean Army, American Army, and every person. God has had enough and will destroy anyone who does not. He is coming to end this war and all wars. You will have two more days to listen and then I will leave this monastery a head to Kaesong. I learned why I was given this power. It is not about me it is about God. He is using me, as God is using you, the Head Monk, my son, and my husband to bring this day and our destiny. God has also used my new son's real mother and father, and an entire city of people to make all this happen." The Priestess read her first transcripts telling her story from her youth and the whole day she continued to read as many as she could. She ended her reading with the first pages of the Bible in Genesis.

Before today's broadcast the Field General had been listening to the radio broadcast with translators and was keeping score. But today he's thinking. She was talking about us, the Army, any army, and she was coming with people with horns not guns. It was inconceivable to anyone who didn't know the Bible. But the Field General knew the Bible and knew it well. He saw the light then instructed his orderlies to find out if there was any Korean Bibles written in existence. They found a 1938 Revision with the Old and New Testament, written in Korean. The General told them, "I want three million copies sent to me yesterday. Tell them to send me whatever they have now, and then keep sending. We will pay in advance for any they do not have printed just keep printing." Then he included, "I also want horns." Then the General said, "By God this is going to be the cheapest battle we ever fought and I don't believe we're going to lose one soldier, but were gone win this war."

Back at the monastery, Three got a bright idea, "What if we have all those pages hand copied? We can handout three thousand pages to three thousand people. Those three thousand people can make three copies each. Then they would keep a copy then pass two out. It would be a chain reaction. Then they would have the Bible and So Young's transcripts." The Head Monk immediately responded, "Those papers are not leaving my sight or the Priestess. They are our only proof and will not be placed in the hands of collectors who only want a small piece of history being made!"

"Thanks" says Three, "You really enjoy this crushing my ego, don't you." The Head Monk responded, "Perhaps." Then the light came on over Three's head again, and said, "Do you suppose there is already a Korean Bible?" The Head Monk poked his head up as if he were an alerted rooster. With wide open eyes he said, "Of course there must be, why haven't I thought of this before? I could have saved my old Bible and been reading and transcribing it for the past fifteen years. With my high education and all that I learned it only gave me enough sense to keep good records. Now I am feeling ignorant." Three inserted, "It's about time." Then the Lieutenant said, "Why don't we ask the General to see if she can find Korean Bibles then send them to us to pass or for that matter just start passing them out from there to here." Three said, "Now why didn't I think of that, now I feel stupid again." Then they called the General and he said, "I'm way ahead of you. I have five hundred thousand bibles already here and two and half million coming behind these. We expect to have all three million here in the next three days. Meanwhile I already have my troops passing out the first batch from here to Seoul or where ever you are. We will meet up with you while passing out these Bibles on their way. My God I feel like Moses, Oh I almost forgot and my orderly just reminded me we got those horns in too, now I feel like Joshua, we're passing them out with the Bibles." Then he said, "That's all," and hung up. The Head Monk and Three acted like cheerleaders after overhearing the General's call. Michael told the Priestess in Korean what was going on. Then everyone went hysterical with happiness.

The next day the Priestess gave her second day broadcast at nine o'clock in the morning. She started by saying, "Good morning, today I will start by telling you miracles that are happening right now as I speak. People are working right now printing the pages in the United States and Korea to give to you Korean Bibles which are the same written transcripts that I have with me right now. I will be explaining how I got these transcripts from my visions. They are not translated with new words, but rewritten from the pages from an American Bible. The words of this American Bible were rewritten in Korean by a man in my vision. He was the man who lived in Korea with his family in a hidden city built by monks over seventy years ago. He was a man of God, a missionary from the United States with his wife and child. They were a family headed to Japan after the war in 1945. But somehow they ended up crash landing off our coast and into the gates of this hidden city."

Then the Priestess started reading the transcripts of her visions of the people in hidden city, the boy, and his father's first writings. As she read she came to a paragraph from Michael's father's memoirs that read, "Its gates were kept closed to protect them, but also keep anyone from leaving into this world. They hid themselves from a world that is known to destroy life and have traits of greed, selfishness, and give rise to truce breakers and warmongers." Then the Priestess commented, "This is the same politics that threatens us now as it did them eighty years ago. History repeats itself over and over and this boy lived in this hidden city. I watched this boy who is now my son growing up there behind those tall stone walls. They never knew any violence, or greed, or selfishness. Everyone in that city only knew love, kindness, and served each other before themselves. They were servants by choice and never asked for anything but kindness in return." Then she read transcripts of the boy and his father the rest of the day. Just before ending her day reading she hesitated to find one of the first pages she read. Finding it, she reread the first line, "Our plane crashed in Korea and they found refuge in this beautiful hidden city." Then she stopped reading and said, "My people, I hope you see by these words today that God is alive. So much has happened to them and has happening to us right now. It's not about me and it's about us. God is coming to end this fighting. I am not afraid to die. I'm afraid to live on like this. Not only I, but my son, my husband, our Head Monk, and witnesses have seen into the flames the other side in paradise. Just like your love ones who are now living in paradise God wants us to be living like this here right now. God does not want anymore of us to die before our time. He has given us the power to see and understand His will. The Bible, from this boy's father's pages, is the word of God. It speaks of two commandments. The first commandment is to love the Lord thy God with all our heart, soul mind and strength. The second commandment is to love your neighbor as yourself. I have been talking to you and all Korea, even China everyday for two days and after my broadcast tomorrow I will leave the following morning heading to Kaesong." She stopped her message there and the Head Monk took over. He said, "We are here, thirty thousand and three hundred thousand line the streets from here to Seoul. Please keep listening to her broadcast. As she pointed out all Koreans, North, South, even China are listening. To the Koreans we know the Priestess as the protector of life. She is only a tool used by God to send you Gods message. Everyone listening will have no excuse not to know or make the right decision including all the forces at war. We will leave here after one more day. We are coming to Kaesong with over one million. Until then, may God bless us and continue to help and teach us."

The third and final day the Priestess only talked a moment before letting Michael tell his story. Michael was almost thirteen but still very naïve. Michael didn't have any pages to read only speaking from his heart. He told his story just as he had told the Lieutenant and Three except all of his stories were spoken in perfect Korean. His words and stories had people laughing and crying.

And Michael left nothing out including Three's few misadventures. Michael even let it known the Priestess was called Three's secret weapon and the "Ark of the Covenant." He told the world the story in the Bible of those who carried it. The General of course was a fan of the Bible and the Priestess and cheered Michael's disclosure. With the cat out of the bag, all the enemy could do is read the Bible to find out what their up against. The General was also becoming a great fan of Three. He was real character but he was also one of the biggest players with the Head Monk and his associates. Afterwards the Priestess came on and said, "Tomorrow you will see me and my new son for the first time. Both of us have been hidden from this world for our own protection. Now our protection is in your hands. We will be leaving for Kaesong to by cart and I want to see every one of you. You will see my son, a young boy with blonde hair who spoke to as if he was born in this country. We both love this country and want to see everyone living in peace. Everyone that has heard me in all Korea, North and South, I urge you to come join God and receive his written word. Let your fight be with yourself and your right to decide. Ask yourselves who can hold your heart and soul your country or your God. This goes for the leaders of this war. I suppose you have a hearts as well. You will have to decide and I believe the Americans have spoken by printing us Korean Bibles and delivering horns. For those that do not align their will with God and His word please understand I am but a messenger of God. He is coming to rapture His people and all those who lay down their weapons. God is coming to destroy those who continue to fight. You will die standing before God. Your life is everlasting. If you follow the high leaders with arms you will lose your life here in this world and your eternal life after death will not be in paradise." The Priestess stopped and the Head Monk spoke momentarily saying, "The Priestess has said every word. I cannot add to anything as she has covered every aspect. Now I will leave you in prayer. May God continue to help us and teach us. Amen."

At the end of the broadcast the General called the Lieutenant and said, "Lieutenant, I want you to ask our Secret Weapon if she will allow us to publish her papers after this things over. If so I'm prepared offer her ninety five percent of the profits." the Head Monk overhearing asked the Priestess. Then the Head Monk dropped his head replying, "The Priestess says you may have ninety five percent. She wants five percent and her papers back undamaged." The

General got disconnected as he fell down along with the Lieutenant, Three, and the Head Monk. Then the Priestess reprimanded them by saying, "Look at all of you. You're already spending my money that I don't want. We never needed money and the little sum we do use is not enough to change the way we live. We live the way we want to live. Those things we need or want God gives us. If He wants me to turn this place or the hidden city into the Taj Mahal then he should have wrote it in His book. The Head Monk and Three looked at each other and were both wondering who ever mentioned the Taj Mahal, then shrugged.

CHAPTER THIRTEEN

OUR SECRET WEAPON

The morning started early with a last minute broadcast and the Priestess saying, "As soon as this last broadcast message is over I will no longer speak, nor will the Head Monk except to greet my people in person. You were instructed to make horns. Yesterday the American Army was passing Korean Bibles and horns to everyone from Kaesong to here. We have none to give but follow us and you will receive them. Right now I want ever person to sound your horns."

No one had any idea how many horns were built or how many horns were handed out until now. The whole of Korea trembled as if a massive earthquake were taking place. And the Priestess fell to her knees in tears. Everyone around her fell to their knees and there was not a dry eye, not even the Head Monk, Three, the Lieutenant, soldiers, and all the monks. Then suddenly the horns all stopped in all directions as the Spirit of God fell over all of Korea. No one in Korea at that point could look up or cry as God placed serenity and spell of calmness that encircled every living thing. Even cars and mechanical equipment seem to go silent. No one spoke or could speak from the heaviness of His being.

Three minutes later the Spirit lifted and everyone found it hard to speak or get back to their feet. "What just happened?" asked the Lieutenant. Three said, "I was wrong. That was Our Secret Weapon." The Lieutenant said, "I don't believe I can handle another attack like this. It was awesome." Then the Priestess gathered herself and said over the radio microphone, "My people every four hours from now you will blow the horns. The Bible says: 'Behold I will come quickly, and my people reward is with me, to give to every man according to his work shall be. God said I am Alpha and Omega, the beginning and the end, the first and the last'."

She continued, "Gods word says, 'Blessed are they that do his commandments that they have the right to the tree of life, and may enter in through the gates into the city.' For those who do not, are dogs, and sorcerers, and whoremongers, and murderers, and idolaters, whosoever loveth and makes a lie. Everyone is for God or if against God will be considered an enemy of God. You have only one option, we leave for Kaesong now."

After her broadcast everyone was prepared to move out. Some of soldiers stayed to breakdown the equipment. The Lieutenant ordered every truck in position and emptied the first truck for the Priestess parked outside the doors. A procession was leaving the temple led by monks carrying the huge trunk. Michael carried the torches behind them, lastly Three and the Priestess watched their every move. The soldiers were waiting and ready to help load the truck. But once outside the Priestess said, "No." Then the monks set the trunk down. The Lieutenant came running asking, "What's wrong." Michael was standing by the Priestess and asked her what she wanted to do. The Priestess said, "Where's my cart." Just then the Head Monk came around the corner and he requests the Lieutenant to move his truck and men. Once the trucked moved he whistled for the first cart. It came around the corner with two pullers and three monks on back. The Head Monk helped the Priestess in the driver's seat then helped Michael in the cart to sit beside her with the torches. He told Three to join the monks on the back. Afterwards he urged the Priestess to pull up and whistled again and a second cart came from around the corner. It too had two pullers and only one extra monk. The Head Monk ordered the huge trunk to be loaded into his cart. Then he got up in the driver seat beside the monk riding shotgun. Priestess ordered the Lieutenant by way off the Head Monk, "Let all our monks march in front your line of empty trucks. Then allow the elderly, handicapped, mothers, babies, and children ride in the trucks and men if there is room. Then they left with the carts up front. The pace was slow as both carts zig zaged across the road to greet people.

As they rode Michael waived the two torches as the Priestess shook hands and greeted her people. She wore her red silk dress with the golden hair pin placed perfectly in her finely combed black hair. As she passed, people raised their horns they made. It wasn't long before she noticed the U.S. Army soldiers coming on foot towards them with Bibles and horns passing them out. The Priestess started crying again when she saw them. Michael hugged her shoulders while Three had his arms around both of them from in back. When four hours came every horn started blowing again. Even Three, Michael, and The Priestess blew horns they received from the soldiers. Again the presence of God came and everything stopped. Every truck, every person, even babies, children, birds, and dogs, stayed silent. It was eerie and the heaviness of

God's Spirit made every head bow, some to their knees, and some were laying flat on the ground facedown. This lasted three minutes then the Spirit of God released His grip. The Lieutenant got out the truck and started throwing up while saying, "God I can't handle this do you have to be so..."then he threw up again.

Back at headquarters the General called for every Chaplin they could reach and the General was bracing himself with his troops every time the horns blew. The same effects were felt all over even in North Korea and their people were in a panic mode. But many of their leaders were still in a fighting mode like Pharaohs in Egypt not backing down. But, every time the horns blew more and more North Koreans left. Even Chinese came by boats across the Yellow Sea. The horns were effective even if they were to far away to hear they were heard about.

At the Generals meeting with his Chaplins he said "We got to make this quick even I'm getting nervous. Are you guys feeling and hearing what I hear, and have you guys kept up with what's going on?" His Head Chaplin said, "We know about the horns, and we know half of Korea headed to Kaesong. But we really not sure why." General said, "Go figure, always my leaders are last to know. Orderly, get those translators in here with the other orderlies that took records of the events for the last two weeks. Especially the last four days. And you Chaplin's brace yourselves in three hours and twenty seven minutes from now. Those horns are going to blow again. Then if you guys haven't notice God's Spirit, it is like wearing a suit of armor and milestone while trying to cross a river of mud. I don't have to dare you to move or say nothing you'll see if you're paying attention. Now you all sit here and listen to these records."

Three and a half hours later the horns blew again and the results were always followed by God's Spirit. This went on day and night every four hours. The General thought of everything he had K rations handed out and Medics standing by with meal and water at stations all along the route. Meanwhile, the Head Monk drove his cart with the trunk full of papers as if they were a New Testament Arch of the Covenant and God was certainly heavily involved in its establishment.

After three days they reached Seoul with estimations of close to two million people and lining the roads to Kaesong. When the General got those figures he ordered more Bibles in Korean and English version and brass horns for his men. On the fifth day it was going to be

Sunday and the General and everyone was wondering what to do. But Sunday morning at midnight The Spirit of God fell and again it brought everyone to their knees and the world around went silent. South Korea, North Korea were stopped in their tracks while a calmness came and it wouldn't allow anyone to speak let alone blow a horn. This was it, the Lords Day. The Spirit of God stayed and never fully lifted. With all of the horns staying silent the people just read their Bibles.

That day and the only head up was the Pharaohs of the North Koreans. The North Korean leaders went over Kim II and received authority from the Chinese leaders to reinforce the DMZ line. With their new power they went a bit further and they put everything they had on the line to Kaesong. Rumors spread fast in the military and by civilians. It was like God was allowing North Koreans to get the upper hand by standing still. When the first news was heard by Sunday afternoon some people were saying, "God led us in a trap and we are all going to be killed!" Or they said, "Are we so sure there really is a paradise for us?" These kind statements were starting up everywhere. Some people threw down their Bibles and said things that hurt and turned people back.

Even the General was under the gun. He had to decide whether or not to fortify the line, to fight them before they came, or wait and fight back if they did open fire. Now since the General had all the Chaplins together he called them in with all his staff and division leaders. Once everyone was assembled, the General started, "I called everyone here and all of you should know why by now. If we put our stuff up against the North, this sends a signal that both armies going to fight this fight as if God did not exist. The people believe God will destroy anyone with a weapon. If we draw our weapons this means we do not believe in God. And if God does not destroy us, being armed to the hilt, the Priestess and the monks will be killed by their own followers. Either way someone is going to die if we do react. Before they put their stuff on the line we had two million plus civilians headed this way and getting stronger. Now today by North Korean Army not honoring Sunday they used our break to call a bluff. I estimate one million civilians dropped out of this crusade because they are scared to die. I can't blame them. I'm not fond of the idea either but my job description says I'm here to die if necessary for what ever reason the United States calls me to defend. Now so much of my patriotic speech. Anyway we have one million die hard civilians coming regardless and they outnumber us ten times. We can't stop them so I got the answer. Behind them I have four and have divisions of men. I want the rest of my divisions ready in dress uniforms, polished boots, and issued every soldier a brass horn. I want everything beautifully polished. I want bugles, trumpets, and saxes, and our best players up front. And I want the word out to all the civilians we are going to fight the way God said to fight and if we die we will go down looking good and playing the blues. Now then we have a lot to do lets get to it. Chaplin's I need to see you a moment longer." The General asked, "Gentlemen, am I crazy? Be honest and feel free to speak your mind." The Head Chaplin asked if they could step aside a minute and have a group huddle. Once the together they talked over the Generals orders. The Head Chaplin said, "General we commend your decision. We could have never been in the position to make this call even if we wanted to. To stake out the lives of so many men as you did and for what? We fight for hills or to gain ground for all kinds of reasons. And we die for those reasons and sometimes not sure what they are. But here we have a reason God said, 'enough is enough' this is a final showdown. The civilians called them out before us showing everyone they have had enough. Now we are saying we will lead you because you led us into to this. By the people willing to risk their lives, we must risk our lives because they have had enough and will not stop. Isn't that true of every war we fight but now we have the best reason of all, God's calling on us to make the same choice as the people. Live together or die together."

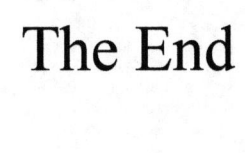